For WWN & Company

BANBURY BOG

Second Printing

, 1966 by Phoebe Atwood Taylor

N 0-88150-090-9

d in 1987 by Foul Play Press, a division
ress, Woodstock, Vermont 05091.

United States of America

D1213804

Also by Phoebe Atwood Taylor
available from Foul Play Press

THE ANNULET OF GILT
THE CAPE COD MYSTERY
THE CRIMSON PATCH
THE MYSTERY OF THE CAPE COD PLAYERS
THE MYSTERY OF THE CAPE COD TAVERN
THE PERENNIAL BOARDER
SANDBAR SINISTER

PHO

B

An

Copyright © 1938

ISE

This edition is published
of The Countryman

All

Printed in the

CHAPTER I

It was while Tabitha Sparrow waited for the Banburys to come that the fog arrived.

The minute she sniffed it, Tabitha groaned. Like other weather-wise Cape Codders, she knew that this fog meant trouble. This fog was going to cause grief.

This was not the slinking, sinister fog that invariably left a drizzling rain in its wake, nor was it the type which East Weesit, borrowing a phrase from carpet-cleaning of another generation, referred to as a Tea Leaf. A Tea Leaf was the regular June fog that slipped in evenings when the sun went down, and slipped out the next morning at sunrise, leaving behind a salty tang in the air, and a fresher, cleaner shade of blue in the sky.

This fog, billowing in so boldly, blotting East Weesit off the map, was the variety Tabitha had learned, during her fifty years, to detest. This was a Stayer. And no one who had not experienced the damp, leisurely course of an East Weesit Stayer could possibly imagine what that meant. Almost anything could happen during a Stayer, and it usually did.

Tabitha sniffed again at the fog, and closed the east door.

Tomorrow that east door, along with every drawer, cupboard and window in her house, would be stuck tighter than a drum. Matches would refuse to light. Spots of mildew would break out on the linens. Sheets would be clammy. Beds would be damp. Even clothes hung carefully away in closets would begin to look crinkly and shapeless. Sooner or later, the dampness would do something to the electricity, and then the plumbing and the water pump would stop. Every sentence would be punctuated by the mournful bellow of the fog horn on Weesit Point. Every five minutes that thing would bellow. Every five minutes, twelve times every hour, twenty-four hours every day, until the fog went out, or until the horn gave out, as it occasionally did. Then they started the siren, which was worse.

If it weren't for the Banburys coming, Tabitha would have taken the fog in her stride. If it were the Abbotts or any of her regular boarders, she would never have given the fog another thought. But these Banburys were new people who had never been on Cape Cod before. They had never seen an East Weesit Stayer. If the fog stayed, as she well knew it would, then the Banburys wouldn't. And with the town taxes steadily mounting, and trade steadily falling off, every boarder counted. These Banburys, who sent long-winded telegrams at the drop of a hat, and made no effort to get rates reduced on a party of three, these Banburys had to stay. They had to stay at least two weeks, until the Abbotts came.

"And," Tabitha said firmly to herself, "they're going to stay!"

Ten minutes later, she marched upstairs to the best bed-rooms and set to work.

She began by putting roses in all the vases, although there was nothing the matter with the daisies and bachelor buttons already there. Her most cherished hooked rug, the one with the full-rigged ship, replaced the rag carpet in the big front room. The simple cotton bedspreads were retired to the linen closet in favor of her best candlewicks, usually reserved for her oldest and most expensive boarders. These three Banburys might turn out to be ink spillers or ash droppers, Tabitha thought, but she'd have to take the chance. Business was business.

As a final gesture, she lighted fires in all the fireplaces, upstairs and down, although it wasn't cold enough to warrant lighting even one. But there was something about open fires that seemed to lull boarders into accepting even a Stayer.

Tabitha sighed as she snapped on the living room lights and sat down to wait.

These gestures hadn't been necessary in the old days, when lines of chauffeurs and town cars stood outside Weesit

Inn, and when Governor Phillips opened the Bog House in April and kept it full of company till late October. In those days, her whole house was booked a year in advance, and she would have laughed at the thought of letting the best rooms, on two days' notice, to complete strangers from the Middle West. But the Inn was closed, now. The shutters hadn't even been taken off in five years. Bog House was falling to pieces, and its once famous rose gardens were a maze of thorns and weeds. The Weesit Yacht Club had disbanded. The Weesit Country Club had become a roadhouse and filling station.

Of all the landmarks that had been Weesit in its prosperous days, only Tabitha Sparrow's remained. She alone had kept her house in repair. She alone had never let down either on the quality of her food or the quality of her guests.

But if these three Banburys didn't stay, Tabitha decided, she would have to give in and cater, like the others, to the overnight tourist trade. She'd have to have every Tom, Dick and Harry clumping in and out, marking up the paneling, scratching the Chippendale, using the pink luster cups for ash trays. She would serve hot dogs and hash and store bread, instead of lobster and prime beef and hot rolls. And she wouldn't make enough money to pay the taxes.

A horn blared outside, and a car turned into the driveway.

Tabitha got up, smoothed out her dress, tucked in a stray strand of white hair, and called to Mary, out in the kitchen.

"They've come, Mary. And don't you forget your cap!"

At the front door, Tabitha paused for a moment by the side glass and surveyed the trio that emerged from the big sedan. Mr. Banbury was a large, massive man, and he topped the six-foot-high carriage light by a good four inches. Mrs. Banbury, whom he helped out of the front seat, was small and bird-like. The tall girl lighting a cigarette was obviously the daughter who had been mentioned in some of the telegrams. She was twenty-two or twenty-three, Tabitha decided, and if the tone of her voice was any indication, she already loathed Cape Cod, violently.

"Yes, yes, Janey, this is it!" Mr. Banbury said. "I know. It's just like Mrs. Sparrow said—what? What's the matter now?"

The girl said something that Tabitha couldn't catch.

"I know it isn't!" Mr. Banbury retorted. "I never said it was a hotel, did I? I said that George Lovell said it was the most comfortable, friendly place he ever stayed in, and the food was the best he ever ate in his life. I never said it was a hotel. It isn't, thank God! No damn swing orchestras, and no damn phony princes, and no damn frills! And as far as you're concerned, Janey, I hope there's not even a goddamn lifeguard on the beach! What you say, Lu?"

"Ssh, dear!" Mrs. Banbury said. "Not so loud, dear! Not so loud!"

"Now listen, Lu," Mr. Banbury made no effort to lower his voice, "here's a place where you can hunt antiques to your heart's content, see? And I'm going to rest. And Janey can just sit right smack on her tail and think about that phony prince—"

"Dad, I think you—"

"Just you don't bother thinking a thing, Janey! You and your mother had your way for a month, and now I'm going to have my way. S'pose there *is* some fog. What of it? You yank out those bags, Janey. Yes, sir. One solid month in that damn hotel you two picked out, and the only folks I ever got to know were the golf pro and the desk clerk, and there wasn't a cup of coffee fit to drink! Janey, yank out those bags. All of 'em. *All* of 'em!"

Tabitha was smiling as she opened the screen door and came out on the top step. It was a genuine, friendly smile, and there was nothing forced about it. Tabitha knew now what Mr. Banbury wanted, and Mr. Banbury was going to get it. And, in her mind's eye, she saw her tax bill, neatly stamped "Paid in Full."

"Welcome to Weesit, Mr. Banbury," she said. "Dinner will be ready just as soon as you've washed up. Welcome to Weesit!"

Mr. Banbury smiled back. He liked the looks of this pleasant-faced, white-haired woman, and he liked the looks of the house. And whatever it was that he smelled cooking, it smelled good.

"Thanks, Mrs. Sparrow," he said. "I guess that we'll—"

"Dad," Jane interrupted, "you don't want every bit of the luggage, do you? The steamer cases, and everything?"

"When I say all the bags," Mr. Banbury told her firmly, "I mean all the bags. All of 'em. We're staying here."

So, as simply as all that, without brass bands or flying flags or any fanfares, the Banbury family arrived in Weesit.

Later, as the summer wore on, it occasionally bothered Tabitha to think that she was the person responsible for their coming, that her food and her open fires and her untiring efforts in their behalf inveigled the Banburys into remaining, despite the Stayer. Nor was she ever completely reconciled by Asey Mayo's consoling suggestion that Phineas Banbury would never have come or have remained, if he had not wanted to. After all, as Tabitha told Asey, she welcomed the man, twice.

But if Tabitha Sparrow was responsible for the Banburys' coming, it was Jane who unwittingly paved the way for her father's actually embracing Weesit. It was Jane who drove Phineas Banbury over to the point on the third day of the Stayer.

Her plan was simplicity itself, and she deliberately chose the point for her setting. The fog was thickest there, and the din of the fog horn was more unbearable and more poignantly mournful than anywhere else. Weesit Point, in short, was definitely the best place to display Weesit at its worst. And, having unsuccessfully tried everything else she could think of to persuade her father to leave, Jane was going to follow her mother's hesitant advice and attempt a little practical psychology. Phineas Banbury was a man who throve on opposition, so Jane was going to make a graceful, capitulating right-about-face, and urge him to stay.

Perhaps, she thought, if his principal opposition wilted, the man might actually look at the fog, listen to that infernal fog horn, and abandon his notion of remaining in what Jane considered the dullest and most godforsaken spot she'd ever been thrust into.

Leaning back against the car seat, Jane lighted a cigarette and listened, without wincing, to the bellow of the horn.

"You know," she said casually, "that noise drove me crazy at first, but now that I'm used to the thing, I don't really mind it at all."

Mr. Banbury threw a half-smoked cigar out of the window, and grunted.

"Damn fog's got in my cigars," he said. "Where did your mother go?"

"To that hooked rug place. They're going to make her a rug like Mrs. Sparrow's. That one with the ship. Momsie's really having a pretty swell time here, dad. She's getting a terrific kick out of those rugs, and the Sandwich glass, and all the stuff she's gone and bought herself."

"Junk," Mr. Banbury said. "Junk. Say, Janey, you got a match that'll light?"

Jane pressed her thumb on the car lighter.

"This still works," she said. "Here. Er—say, dad."

"Uh-huh."

Mr. Banbury, who knew every intonation of his daughter's voice, looked at her sharply out of the corner of his eye as he lighted a fresh cigar.

"Dad," Jane didn't notice his quick glance, "dad, I owe you an apology. I've been scrimy since we came here. Perfectly scrimy."

Mr. Banbury nodded thoughtfully.

"Yes," he said, "you certainly have, Janey. You've gone right through your bag of tricks. I told your mother last night that if you kept it up, I was going to ship you back to St. Louis and set you to work at the dough mixers. And let me tell you, that'd be a lot worse than Cape Cod in the fog."

"Well," Jane said defensively, "there's so *much* fog, dad. That's what's got me down!"

"No," Mr. Banbury said, "it's not. You were down before you got here. That phony prince got you down. Honestly, Janey, you should have known that fellow was no prince! I knew he was a barber, right away. He looked like a barber, and he smelled like one. You better get onto yourself, Janey. As long as Banbury's tarts keep rolling out of the ovens of seventeen factories, you're going to have plenty of hungry-looking guys wanting you to elope in the moonlight with 'em—"

He paused while the horn bellowed.

"And half of 'em," he continued as the bellow died away, "will be counts, at least. Janey, that horn's beginning to get under my skin. And will you look at this cigar? Out again. And do you know what? My shoes were all full of green mold this morning. Just like an old cheese. But it wiped right off. Yes, Janey, you better get onto yourself. I won't ride you any more about your prince. I'll forget him—"

"Thank you, darling," Jane jumped at her opportunity. "And will you forget all the things I've said about Cape Cod? And about this town? I never meant any of them. And Mrs. Sparrow says it's a darling town, really. Of course, we've never got a chance yet to see the place, but I shouldn't have gone around taking cracks at it, just because of the fog. I'm not really having such a hideous time. I think it might be fun to stay here."

The fingers of Mr. Banbury's right hand beat a little tattoo on the car door.

"Really, Janey?" he said. "You mean that?"

"Yes," Jane said, "I do. I think it might be fun to stay, even if the fog stays nineteen days. Mrs. Sparrow said that it did, once."

Jane darted a look at her father, and decided suddenly to go all the way and give him the works.

"You know," she said, "I bet a man like you could do a lot for a little town like this."

She knew, somehow, before she finished speaking, that she had made some sort of mistake. Her mother had warned her about going too far and urging him too much. And Phineas Banbury, when he turned around, had a gleam in his eye and that expression on his face which her mother always called his Guess-I'll-start-a-new-factory look.

"Janey," he said earnestly, "do you really think so?"

"Well," Jane began, "I think you—"

"Good!" Mr. Banbury said. "You do, don't you? Well, I hadn't told your mother—in fact, I've kept this a secret from the two of you, but now that you've brought it up yourself, I'll tell you the whole thing. You know, I'd been sort of wondering in the last hour if I hadn't better give up and go, Janey. Your mother seems happy enough here, but when you're out of sorts, you get her all worked up, and there's always her blood pressure. And then there's been this damn fog, fog, fog, everywhere, in my shoes and my cigars and my clothes. But—well, you really want to know why I insisted on coming here?"

He went on before Jane could manage to answer him.

"Well, when I was a little kid, great-uncle Phineas Knowles—he's the one I was named for—he used to live with us. And he came from this town, did you know? Yes, sir, he stayed here with relations and was brought up right here in this town. Well, he used to sit on the back porch when I was a kid, and tell me all about this town, and the ocean—I'd never seen the ocean, then, you know. It was just the blue part of the map, to me. Anyway, he used to tell me how he was going to make a fortune, and come back, and do things for this town. Had it all planned, what he was going to do. Then he died—that was when I was sixteen—and he left me what money he had. And do you know what I did with that money?"

Jane shook her head.

"Well, with that money," Mr. Banbury said, "I set up my first bakery. Yes, sir, the first Banbury tarts came from that little bakery I got from the money that great-uncle Phin left me. And do you know what I said to myself, all through the years?"

Jane drew a long breath.

Knowing Phineas Banbury, she had a very good idea of what he had said to himself, and the thought of it sent shivers running up and down her spine. If only her mother were here! Lu Banbury would have known exactly what to answer. Without riling Phineas, she could have nipped the whole business in the bud, right then and there.

"I'll tell you what I said," Mr. Banbury mistook Jane's hesitancy for lack of imagination, "I said, when I made money, I'd go back to that little Cape Cod town, and I'd do all the things that great-uncle Phin wanted done. That's just what I said. I never told a soul, either. Not even your mother. When I retired, I had this town on my mind. That was why I said I'd take a real vacation and come east with you last month. You two sort of delayed me, at that damn hotel, but this was where I intended to come. Yes, sir, Janey, I'm glad you changed your mind about wanting to go. I'm glad you really like this place. Because, by George, I'm going to stay, and—say, isn't that the sun?"

"No." Jane felt too defeated to bother turning her head to investigate. "No. Sometimes it just looks lightish, but it doesn't mean a thing. Dad, don't you think maybe you better consult with mother, and sort of mull over the topic of great-uncle Phin before you start—"

"One thing about your mother," Mr. Banbury said, "I can count on her. She always likes to do what I want to do. It's just you that makes all the trouble. And now you're all settled. You like this place. You said so. You were just

up at the crossroads the day before. That accident was one of the things that sent Phineas bustling up to settle about the traffic lights.

There were three cars left, two beachwagons and a truck. Each carried on its doors the insignia that Jane and Evan had thought up, that sprig of cranberries with "Banbury Bog," in red letters, encircling it. Mrs. Banbury hated beachwagons, but she backed out the nearest one and set off to call on Tabitha Sparrow.

More and more, Mrs. Banbury had come to rely on Tabitha for advice, companionship and information. It was Tabitha who had known at first glance which furniture was genuine and which was fake. It was Tabitha who produced Evan Chase, without whom nothing would ever have got done. She had also produced Judge Chase, Evan's uncle, who had settled all the tangle of legal matters concerning Bog House with what amounted to a wave of his hand. Tabitha had produced a cook, and maids. She had found carpenters, masons, painters, well-diggers, plumbers, gardeners. And boat builders and tennis court makers and a woman who did hemstitching. And, when Phineas occasionally seemed to be going too far, it was Tabitha who firmly told him as much without any mincing of words. And, miraculously, Phineas took her advice. He even said it was sound.

Tabitha, Mrs. Banbury thought as she parked the beachwagon by Tabitha's orchard, was an invaluable individual.

She was even at home, and free, when Mrs. Banbury wanted her most.

"How nice of you to come over, Lu," Tabitha said. "I was just going to phone you. Come into the garden and Mary'll bring us out some tea. The Abbotts and the Carlyles and the Potters have all gone to the back shore with a picnic supper. Unless you've got a lot of other plans, we might go off and have dinner together, you and I. I want to find out what this woman in Orleans does to her food that makes everyone rave so about it. And I want—" Tabitha paused. "Lu, you seem worried. What's the matter?"

"I wish," Mrs. Banbury said rather wistfully, "that I knew. Tabitha, you'll probably laugh at me, but there's something awfully wrong. About the town, and Phineas. I've just begun to notice it this week, and it's bothering me, terribly. It's nothing definite, at all. It's just this sort of feeling I've got that something is wrong."

Tabitha looked at her steadily for a moment, and then took her arm.

"Come into the garden, Lu," she said. "Come over here and sit down. There. No one'll disturb us here, and we can talk. So you've noticed it, too!"

"Too?" Mrs. Banbury said. "You mean, you know there's something wrong, too?"

Tabitha nodded.

"Yes," she said, "I've been feeling there's something wrong for—oh, for a week or more. I can't explain it. And I'd never in the world have gone to you or Phineas and told you, because I was afraid that you might laugh at me. But now that you've got the same feeling, maybe you and I can figure it out."

"I hope so!" Mrs. Banbury sighed. "Tabitha, I've tried for two days to think this thing out by myself, and put it into words. But I can't. It's just about Phineas. It's the way people talk to him. It's something in the tone of their voices. It's something in the way they listen to him. It's just little things like that. Tabitha, what is the matter? What has Phineas done?"

Tabitha got up from her canvas chair, and looked thoughtfully down the hillside at the town. Her eyes were bright when she turned back to Mrs. Banbury.

"What's he done?" she said. "There it is, right in front of you. All of it. The new gilt dome of the church, the new sidewalks, the new trash cans, the new signs, the fresh paint, the window boxes, the tourist bureau. It's all there. The new Whaling Museum in the old sail loft. The new Weesit Yacht Club. The Weesit Inn and the Weesit Country Club, both open again and both filled with the carriage trade as they used to be. Bog House—Banbury Bog—looking the way it used to look. My house, filled with people. That's what he's done."

"Yes," Mrs. Banbury said. "But—"

"D'you know," Tabitha said, "the night you came, I was so desperate that I was ready to go in for the tourist trade if you didn't stay? D'you know that this is the first summer in five years that I've really made any money? D'you realize that this is the first time in five years that anyone in town has made a single cent? What's Phineas

Banbury done? What hasn't he done! He's taken this town, and he's put it back on its feet. That's what he's done!"

"Yes," Mrs. Banbury said gently, "I know all that, Tabitha. And he's had a lot of fun fixing things up, and getting them going. And he's really made money, you know. The Inn and the Club have paid back all he put into things. He says the town just needed capital and a push. But what's he done that's wrong? Could it be the Welcome Wagon? Has that annoyed people?"

Tabitha shook her head.

"The Welcome Wagon's given the town more publicity than anything else," she said. "Ever since it got cartooned in the Boston papers, people talk about it constantly. Everyone who comes to town yells for their free Banbury pie and their free Banbury tarts. People love that Welcome Wagon, and it's brought a lot of trade to town. No, it's not the wagon, I'm sure."

"Well, then," Mrs. Banbury said, "what is it? What's changed people toward Phineas? Everyone used to wave, and ask me how he was, and stop and chat. But lately they haven't. And they always spoke of him as Mr. Banbury of Banbury Bog, or Mr. Banbury of Bog House, but yesterday I heard someone ask what that crazy madman up at the point had thought of now. When did he go too far, Tabitha? Everyone was so friendly and co-operative, and things were going so beautifully—of course, Phineas would say that they still were. He hasn't noticed, yet."

"What's his latest?" Tabitha inquired.

"Those traffic lights. He's up in Boston with Bearse and Abner Grove today, getting some official okay on them. But everyone wants those lights. And really, I can't think of a thing he's done, or got done, that people didn't want. What *is* the matter?"

Tabitha sat down in the canvas chair and wrinkled her forehead.

"I can't think of one single thing," she said. "In fact, I can't even say that there's anything really wrong, now. But I do know I've felt that people had a different attitude toward him and his projects lately, and it's worried me. No one has anything against him—lord knows they've got every reason to be as grateful to him as I am! And no one's said anything against him. But people just seem to feel differently."

"I've been wondering," Mrs. Banbury said, "if it could be the sort of thing that seems to happen so often in politics. You know, at first everyone always says how perfectly splendid the new governor or the new president is, and everything he does is so fine. And then there always seems to come a day when everyone starts calling him That Madman in the Capitol. My father was simply devoted to Teddy Roosevelt, but after a while he got purple in the face at the mention of his name."

Tabitha smiled. "I don't think there's been time enough for that," she said. "Lu, what about Jane? Could she have done anything?"

"Jane," Mrs. Banbury said, "has really been very good this summer. I must say, she's behaved herself amazingly well. The Cape's done her good. She hasn't fallen in love with a single groom or lifeguard or waiter, or anything like that. She's just gone around with Evan Chase, and then only to get things for the house, like chasing that mantelpiece. And Jane looks on Evan as an elderly man with one foot in the grave. He's thirty-one."

"But couldn't she have offended someone?" Tabitha asked. "I'm sure I'd have heard of it if she did, but mightn't she?"

"Jane has been so sunny and so agreeable," Mrs. Banbury said, "that it's inspired Phineas to ask me if I thought she was well. She's helped him a lot, and she's gone to all the fairs and bazaars, and she's helped with the tournaments at the Club, and given prizes, and she goes and reads to those old ladies at Nauset Neck, every other day. No, I'm sure it's not Jane. Or me."

"You've been impeccable," Tabitha said. "In fact, you've been so impeccable that nobody realizes how much of what Phineas gets done is due to you."

"No," Lu Banbury said, "what Phineas does is all his own. I've been glad he's been so happy here, because it's taken his mind off retiring. Of course, he's retired before, but I think he means it this time, and I want him to be busy, and happy."

"His peace of mind matters to you," Tabitha said.

"It matters," Mrs. Banbury said simply, "more than anything else in the world."

Tabitha got up again from the canvas chair, and strolled over to the apple tree. Tabitha was a little fidgety today,

Mrs. Banbury thought. All this jumping up and down and walking around wasn't like her at all.

"I was thinking," Tabitha said, "of Duncan Sparrow. My husband. He was a large man, rather like Phineas, and I don't think his mind was ever at peace, about anything. He was a minister, and he took the world very seriously. The less peace he had, the better he liked it. Lu, suppose I talk to Abner Grove about this, and see if he knows anything that might have happened. I'm seeing Judge Chase tomorrow morning, and I'll speak to him about it. Suppose you ask Marian Milton—no, perhaps I'd better. Those women who make her rugs hear everything, and they chatter incessantly while they work. She'll know, if there is anything. Lu, maybe it's just the reaction of prosperity."

"Maybe." But Lu Banbury didn't sound as though she really meant it. "But suppose this keeps on, Tabitha? Suppose this sort of attitude we've noticed turns into something else? Suppose people start being unpleasant, and making things unpleasant?"

"If that happens," Tabitha said, "we can always call on my cousin, Asey Mayo. I think he's back—he's been cruising on Bill Porter's yacht."

"Asey Mayo—oh, the detective one? The man they call the hayseed sleuth? Oh, Phineas always reads every word about him in the papers! He's been wanting to meet him."

"Well, let's hope that they'll never have to meet other than socially," Tabitha said. Then, as she saw the look on Lu Banbury's face, she added hastily, "I don't mean that! Don't jump to conclusions! Lu, maybe your husband's peace of mind means so much to you, and maybe I feel so grateful to him, that you and I notice things when they don't exist. Come on, let's go to Orleans and find out what that woman puts in her Indian pudding—speaking of food, isn't it tomorrow that there's the big supper at the East Weesit church?"

"Yes," Mrs. Banbury said. "They're going to try to raise the rest of the money they need for the new electric organ pumper. That pumper is a cause very dear to Phineas's heart, because his great-uncle Phin used to pump the old bellows, by hand. So it's going to be a very special supper, and Phineas is going down to the bakery and make the dessert tarts himself. I must remember to have Anna call me early."

"Call you? Are you going to make tarts, too?"

"Dear me, yes, I've made millions. I worked in the first bakery. Why," Mrs. Banbury said with quiet pride, "I thought up the thumbprint trademark, and the machine that thumbprints all our tarts. Of course, an engineer really built the machine, but it was my own idea. Well, Phineas certainly can't hurt anyone's feelings by baking a few hundred tarts. And Labor Day's coming, and they tell me everyone goes home then. I'm sure, if Phineas thinks it over, he'll have to go home too, and see how things are getting on. Whatever the trouble is, if there is any, I suppose it'll blow over."

"Of course! How Phineas would laugh at us," Tabitha said, "worrying so seriously about something so vague! Will you mind taking the beachwagon? It's probably more reliable than my sedan. That's fine. You wait here till I phone those people in Hyannis about their rooms, and get my coat and hat—"

While she waited, Mrs. Banbury strolled around the garden and thought how much better people felt after talking their problems over with someone. Tabitha was very likely right. Both of them were silly to worry so over something so vague. It was foolish to feel that someone was laying a plot against Phineas, just because people didn't seem to treat him with respectful awe. After all, people were getting to know him, and naturally they wouldn't be as formal as they had been.

Suddenly, Mrs. Banbury became aware of the small figure in overalls that knelt furtively beside the rear tire of the beachwagon, parked just beyond the picket fence.

She knew what the child was doing even before she heard the quick hiss of escaping air.

That right rear tire was flat as a pancake.

Mrs. Banbury started to call out, but before she could utter a word, the child got to his feet, walked over to the door, and thumbed his nose at the cranberry sprig insignia.

Then he ran.

Without hesitation, Mrs. Banbury started after him.

But the realization that he was being pursued seemed to put wings on the child's heels. He was out of sight when Mrs. Banbury turned the corner of the lane and bumped, breathlessly, into the arms of selectman Abner Grove.

"That wretch!" Mrs. Banbury said. "Where'd he go?"

"What wretch? What's the matter, Mrs. Banbury? What wretch?"

"That wretched boy! Oh, dear, I never ran any faster! Oh, did I hurt you when I bumped? I was so intent on getting that child, I didn't see you. Where'd he go?"

"I didn't see any child," Grove said. "I just was starting up the lane when you—uh—came."

"I suppose he turned the other way—oh, would I like to get my hands on him! The wretch just let all the air out of my rear tire! Mr. Grove, this may seem a strange time to ask you, but what has happened about my husband?"

Abner Grove looked at her and blinked, and Mrs. Banbury thought impatiently what a thoroughly ineffectual man he was. She never liked men with stoop shoulders and pale blue eyes, anyway, and at the moment Mr. Grove seemed what Jane called more hemmy-and-hawey than ever.

"My husband, Phineas Banbury," she said. "I want to know, what's the reason for small boys letting the air out of his tires, and thumbing their noses—his nose—well, you know what I mean. What are little boys thumbing their noses at him for?"

"Oh," Grove said. "I thought you meant something else. I—"

"What else?" Mrs. Banbury demanded.

"Oh, it's nothing, really." Grove looked over her head. "Er—if somebody's tampered with your tire, I'd be very glad to fix it for you. Really, I would. I'm sure the child didn't mean anything vicious, or anything like that. I'm sure. Really. Er—children do strange things. That is, if he let the air out of your tire, he probably just did it to annoy you."

"That," Mrs. Banbury said crisply, "was what I gathered. I didn't think he did it to please me and make me laugh. I don't for an instant think he was prompted by any desire to be helpful."

"I'll fix it," Grove said hurriedly. "I'll fix it right away. Yes, right now. Right away."

"That's very kind of you," Mrs. Banbury said, blocking his way. "But first, you stop and tell me what the matter is."

"Well, your husband and I just had a little argument,"

Grove said, and Mrs. Banbury couldn't tell whether or not he had purposely misunderstood her question. "But it was nothing. Nothing at all. Just a little difference of opinion we had on the way back from Boston. Not really an argument. Just a difference, that's all. Er—sometimes your husband is—er—well, a little hard to convince."

"Phineas Banbury, if rightly handled," Mrs. Banbury retorted, "is the most tractable man in the world. What did you fight about on the way back from Boston?"

"Oh, we didn't fight. Not really. Er—it really doesn't matter, Mrs. Banbury. I've already forgotten. I really have. And now, I'll fix your tire—I see Tabitha there, waving to you—"

He managed to pass by her, and from a standpoint of elapsed time, Mrs. Banbury thought, Abner Grove covered the distance up the lane fully as quickly as had that wretched child. Although, of course, Abner Grove didn't really run. He simply gave the impression of flight.

Slowly, Mrs. Banbury followed.

She knew now that she and Tabitha hadn't been so very silly. Something was wrong, and Abner Grove knew it, too. So did that wretched child. Children didn't do things like that unless they'd heard people talking. If he'd just let the air out of the tire and run away, that could have been summed up as mischief, and youthful exuberance. But that nose-thumbing gesture put a different aspect on the situation.

Yes, something was very wrong, and Abner Grove knew, and Tabitha—Mrs. Banbury stopped short and her slight figure stiffened. She felt rather as if someone had poured a cup of ice water down her back.

Of course, Tabitha really knew, too! Tabitha and Abner Grove were great friends. Jane had brought back the information weeks ago that Weesit expected Tabitha and Abner to marry, sooner or later.

Of course, Tabitha knew! She must know, Mrs. Banbury decided swiftly. All that talk about getting Asey Mayo had meant something. It was all clear, now. Tabitha had first tried to find out how much Mrs. Banbury knew, and then, finding that she really didn't know anything that could be classified as a fact, Tabitha had passed the whole thing off and pretended that they were both being silly, and making mountains out of molehills. And—

"Lu!" Tabitha called to her. "Abner's got your tire pumped up! It's all fixed!"

Mrs. Banbury hesitated, and then she hurried over toward the beachwagon.

"All done?" she said pleasantly. "Oh, that's so kind of you, Mr. Grove! Tabitha, I'm afraid we'll have to call our dinner party off. I didn't expect Phineas back till late, and now that he's home, I feel I should go—just when did you get back, Mr. Grove?"

"About half an hour ago," Grove told her, looking at his watch. "Maybe thirty-five minutes—"

"Oh, as long as that!" Mrs. Banbury had been prepared to make the same answer if Grove had told her five minutes. "As long as that! Oh, I've got to hurry—you understand, don't you, Tabitha? I'll see you tomorrow—no, I've got to make those tarts with Phineas tomorrow. Well, I'll phone you, then—good-by!"

Back at Banbury Bog, she found Phineas basking comfortably on the west porch.

"Hi, Lu," he said. "Come sit down and look at this view. Look at those yachts—aren't they pretty?"

"Beautiful, dear." She had never, Mrs. Banbury thought. seen a happier, less troubled man. "Did you have a good trip?"

"Uh-huh." Phineas yawned. "Got those lights okayed. Putting 'em in tomorrow. Gee, that's a tiresome ride. All those curves." He yawned again, and then he laughed. "Grove knew this short cut, and if it hadn't been for that, we'd have been home an hour and a half ago. He couldn't make up his mind about the turns to take."

"Phineas, what do you think of Grove?" Mrs. Banbury said. "I mean, what do you *really* think?"

"Oh, he's honest," Phineas said, "and I think he's fond of the town and wants it to get along. He's got more brains than the other two selectmen, but that's not saying much. He hasn't any push to him, but if he'd had any, of course he wouldn't have been content to stay stuck here. I don't know, Lu. He's all right. I'd like him better if he could ever make up his mind. And when he does finally decide, he hems and haws so—gets on my nerves."

"Phineas, have you been bullying him?"

"You can't bully a man like Grove," he said. "You just have to wait till he stops teetering and wavering, and makes up his mind. He got me kind of sore, bumping over his old short cut, but I never bullied him."

"I wonder," Mrs. Banbury began tentatively, "I wonder, Phineas, what you—"

"Look at the bay now, Lu—see the boats? They're just making the buoy. Now that's a lovely sight, Lu. Honestly, this is a lovely view. And it's a lovely house. By George, Lu, I've had a good time this summer, and I think the townspeople like what we've got done, too, don't you? But I've been thinking, maybe we better run home after Labor Day—what was it you were wondering about a second ago?"

Mrs. Banbury surveyed the view, and her husband, and the placid, contented glow on his face.

She hated to disturb that glow. And, besides, if they went home after Labor Day, there really wasn't any sense in disturbing him and getting him all worked up about something that was still vague and nebulous, even if she were sure of it.

"I was wondering that, too," she said. "I think we should go home before the directors' meeting. Charley is good, but I think you should keep an eye on things just the same."

Phineas yawned.

"That's what I thought. Well, after this supper tomorrow, we'll make plans, and see what Jane wants to do this fall. We better turn in early tonight, Lu. We got those tarts to make tomorrow. Of course, they'll never get enough money from the supper to pay for the organ pumper, and I'll fork over the difference, and it'd be easier if I just gave 'em a check. But these folks like things better if they have a hand in 'em. I'm going to make cherry tarts, Lu. Cherry, and peach. And if I do say so, there's no man living can make better cherry tarts or peach tarts than I can."

The two hundred people who jammed the auditorium of the little East Weesit church the next evening concurred with that opinion.

By six-thirty, when the supper was over, seventy dozen tarts had been devoured. Summer people, tourists and natives all agreed that the Banbury tarts made by the bakery and distributed free by Banbury's Welcome Wagon were good tarts. But the tarts made personally by Banbury himself, those were the tarts of a master.

A few hours later, that estimate of Banbury's skill had undergone a violent upheaval.

The first two cases were children. Dr. Dewey, the Weesit physician, diagnosed their ailment as simple indigestion, brought on by an over-indulgence in Banbury tarts.

With the tenth case, Dr. Dewey changed his diagnosis and called in Dr. Cummings from Wellfleet, and Dr. Penn from Pochet. With the fiftieth case, practically the whole of Cape Cod knew.

Like wildfire, the word flew around.

Phineas Banbury had put poison in the tarts he made for the church supper. All of East Weesit was ill. Some embellished the story by adding that all of East Weesit was dying like cattle, and some said that all of East Weesit was dying like flies.

With a poker face, Phineas Banbury listened to the diagnosis of arsenic poisoning, and then he nodded briefly.

"How serious?" he demanded.

Dr. Dewey, whose professional reputation was more or less at stake, shrugged, and shook his head, but Dr. Cummings of Wellfleet spoke up reassuringly.

"Don't worry, Mr. Banbury," he said. "I've seen worse trouble from lobster. A little arsenic's good for the blood. We'll fix 'em up."

"Get everything you need," Phineas said. "Anything. Charge it all to me. Send all the bills to me. I'll be at my house if anyone wants me."

At the door, he paused and crooked his finger at Dr. Cummings, who came over to him.

"Don't worry, Mr. Banbury. Nobody's going to die. Just don't listen to—"

"Yes," Phineas said, "I believe you. What I want to know is, how do I get hold of Asey Mayo?"

"He's over at Bill Porter's for dinner," Cummings said. "I know, because I was there, too, when Dewey called me. If you're meaning to get hold of him, I think you're doing the wise thing."

"I know damn well I am!" Phineas said, and strode out to where Jane and Lu waited in the car.

"Arsenic poisoning, from the tarts," he informed them. "They're claiming I stuffed those tarts full of arsenic. Of all the crazy things! But anyway, I'm glad this business's come out into the open. Now that I know where I stand, I can do something."

"You mean," Lu said slowly, "you knew—"

"Oh, I knew someone was gumming up the works. I knew something was going on," Phineas said. "That's why I said that about going home, yesterday. I didn't want to get you worked up. I was thinking about your blood pressure. Yes, sir, I said to myself there was a plot against me, and by George, here it is! I—what are you giggling about, Janey? This isn't anything to giggle about!"

"Momsie," Jane said, "were *you* keeping it from *him?* You were! Well, so were Evan and I. We knew there was something up when we heard people calling me Banbury's tart. And—"

"They did, did they?" Phineas said. "And you both knew. Huh. Lu, I'm going to get Abner Grove. He knows something about this. You and Jane go over to Bill Porter's in Wellfleet and bring Asey Mayo back here. You tell him someone's trying to get me in wrong and drive me out of Weesit, and that they're scattering arsenic over my tarts and saying I did it. You tell him I don't care what it costs, I want to find out who's responsible, and I want him to find out just as soon as he can—"

"Dad," Jane broke in, "are they sure about the arsenic? I just can't believe that! Don't you suppose it's just because those pigs stuffed themselves so?"

"No, Dr. Cummings said it was arsenic, and he seems to know his business. And you see how damn bad it looks! *We* aren't sick!"

"But we never ate any tarts!" Jane said. "We never do!"

"You and I haven't eaten a tart in thirty years," Lu added indignantly, "except in the line of business sampling. You know that, Phineas!"

"I know, I know! But you see how it looks to outsiders! Now, you two go get Asey Mayo, and bring him back to the house. I'll get Grove, and we'll set to work on this. And to think I was sparing you! Oh, get going, Janey! Hurry!"

Phineas was pacing restlessly up and down the west porch when Jane and Mrs. Banbury returned to Banbury Bog an hour later.

"Where's Asey Mayo?" he asked. "Where is he? Wouldn't he come?"

"He's coming," Jane said. "He stopped off at Dewey's to talk with that Dr. Cummings—dad, he looks just like his pictures, tall and lean and sort of tanned and weather-beaten. And he's got a Porter sixteen roadster that looks like a centipede on wheels. And—"

"He's awfully nice, Phineas," Lu said. "So pleasant and helpful. He came right away. And, dear, I don't think I'd mention fees. I think I'd just ask him to help—"

"Listen, Lu," Phineas said loudly, "I don't care what he looks like or what he drives, or anything else! I just want him! I want—is that Asey Mayo?"

He pointed to the tall man who was getting out of the rakish roadster that had slid quietly up to the foot of the garden path.

"Is that him?" Phineas said again. "But he's all dressed up in flannels! He doesn't look that way in pictures! He—"

Mrs. Banbury sshed, but Asey had heard the comment, and he was grinning as he came up on the porch.

"You caught me at a party," he said. "I'm not usually so white flannelly. Mr. Banbury, I understand you're havin' some difficulties."

"Difficulties! Say, Mr. Mayo, we're having trouble! And it isn't just those two hundred people all poisoned from those tarts. It's Abner Grove—I can't find him! No one's seen him since he took the tarts over to the church in the Welcome Wagon. Nobody can find him. He's just disappeared from sight! He, and the wagon. Both of 'em gone!"

"You mean that white delivery truck?" Asey inquired. "The one with 'Welcome to Weesit' on the side? Seems to me it would be kind of hard to get lost in that, Mr. Banbury."

"Well, he's gone just the same," Phineas said, "and so's the wagon. And I want him. He knows something about this! And if you want to know what I think, I think it's sort of queer he should disappear right after this arsenic business. Yes, by George, I want to get hold of Abner Grove!"

"S'pose," Asey said, "that you and I take my car and hunt him up, Mr. Banbury. He may just be stuck on some back road with engine trouble, or something like that—"

"The Welcome Wagon was checked at the garage yesterday," Phineas said, "and it's got two spares. And if there'd been an accident, we'd know it."

"Well," Asey said, "suppose we hunt him up. And while we're doin' that, you can tell me what's been goin' on. I've picked up most of the story from Mrs. Banbury and your daughter and Doc Cummings—"

"And when we find Grove," Phineas said, "I think we'll find out more. Come on—"

It was well after midnight when they finally found Abner Grove, not half a mile from Phineas Banbury's house.

He was sitting in Banbury's Welcome Wagon, down by the outermost edge of the bog, and he was dead.

Behind him on the racks of the Welcome Wagon were trays of the poisoned tarts, and there were still more beside him on the seat.

But, as Dr. Cummings informed them briskly later that night, Abner Grove had not been poisoned.

Abner Grove had been drowned.

an anyone ever did in twenty years. He hasn't
thing that hasn't been popular, as far as I can
. He hasn't done anything that wasn't all to the
hasn't strutted around and asked for praise. He's
the credit to the people and the selectmen. Now
hell did somebody go and stick that arsenic in his
hat's the big idea? And," Cummings went on be-
ey had a chance to answer, "and, furthermore, in
what he's done for 'em, and what a fine man they
t he was yesterday, do you know that every last
in that benighted town of Weesit actually believes
anbury poisoned the tarts himself?"

es," Asey said, "I know. Jennie's been doing a little
sdroppin' on her party line, an' she reports that they're
y bitter about him."

ummings glared at the cream pitcher.

Fools!" he said. "My God, aren't people fools, Asey?
metimes I'm amazed with people for the heights they
n reach, like old Jimmy Smith's rescuing that kid from
e live wire over in Orleans the other day. And then again,
seems to me that people are the damnedest fools! Think
f it. Yesterday, Banbury was the finest man in Weesit.
Then some arsenic gets into some tarts. Do they use their
beans and say it's an accident, or that Banbury is the last
person who'd do such a thing, and so it must have been
someone trying to put Banbury in a hole? No. Overnight
they change their minds and say Banbury's a dirty skunk
that tried to poison a whole town. Overnight!"

"No," Asey said, "I don't agree with that overnight part,
doc. I think this's been goin' on for some time. I gathered
as much from Banbury and Mrs. Banbury. They've noticed
that people have acted different. Nothin' you could put
your finger on, in one sense. Just a sort of change in their
attitudes, like."

"Propaganda, you mean?"

Asey nodded.

"I think so. And little things. Like some kid lets the
air out of Mrs. Banbury's tire, and thumbs his nose at
the little curlicue on the door of the beachwagon. And the
daughter gets catcalls when she goes by. And Banbury says
there've been little arguments, like, about things that don't
matter. Yes, I think there's been some propaganda, and

months th
done any
make ou
good. He
given all
why in
tarts? V
fore A
spite o
thoug
perso
that
"
eave
pret
C
"
So
ca
th
it
o

CHAPTER III

ASEY MAYO,
usual corduroys and canvas jacket, was ea
in his home in Wellfleet when Dr. Cummin
at half-past eight the next morning.

"Hi, doc, sit down and have some coffee—"

"Asey," Cummings said irritably, "how do
Your head hasn't touched a pillow all night, and
like a damn daisy! You're even genial. You see
about the whole thing—man, how do you do it?"

"It's just my years of clean livin'," Asey said
right thinkin'. Have some of Jennie's coffee, doc, a
me about things. How's the poisoning cases, and wha
pened after I left? What did Penn have to say?"

"The poisoning cases are perfectly all right," Cumm
said. "Where's the cream? Thanks. Everyone's all rig
except two couples from Pochet Center who claim they
going to die within the hour."

"Are they?"

"Hell, no!" Cummings said explosively. "They weren't
even at the supper, Penn found out. They're just trying to
work up something to sue Banbury about, that's all! Asey,
I think this is the hell of a business! I like that fellow
Banbury!"

"So do I," Asey returned. "And I think he's been shoved
into as tough a spot—"

"Why?" Cummings interrupted. "Why, for God's sakes?
What're they trying to do? Now there's a man who's put
a town on its feet. He's done more for Weesit in two

it's one of the things I'm goin' to look into before Banbury runs into some real difficulties. Doc, what about Grove?"

"Penn's seen him, and Crandall, that new medical examiner, he came just after you left. There's no question about Grove. I knew the minute I saw him that he hadn't been poisoned. And Crandall and I couldn't find a trace of arsenic in him, Asey. Crandall'll go into the matter more, of course, but I'm positive that the man never ate even a single tart. I'm positive. Besides, Dewey said that he'd put Grove on a strict diet this spring, and all pastry was out. Dewey said that Grove hadn't touched pastry or candy or sweets for months. Yes, Grove was drowned, all right. There was water in his lungs— Asey, how the hell did you catch on to that?"

"Well," Asey said, "he was dead when Banbury and I found him. There wasn't any two ways about that. And he wasn't shot, or stabbed, and he didn't look like he'd been poisoned. Then I spotted that lump on the back of his head, and I thought at first that someone had taken a crack at him. Then I saw those stains on his shirt and collar. Blue stains that'd run from his blue necktie. And his hair was damp, and his collar and the tie was soaking wet. There you are."

Cummings lighted a cigar and puffed at it thoughtfully.

"I still can't see why you thought he was drowned, Asey. Why didn't you just think that he'd been hit over the head with a bucket full of water?"

"The car was dry," Asey pointed out. "And his shoulders and coat and the rest of him was all dry as a bone. And there was something about him that just made me think drowned. I've seen drowned people before, and he looked drowned."

Cummings shook his head.

"My God, this is a mess!" he said. "Drowned, in that car! If you figure this one out, you're going to be good."

"There's nothin' to figure," Asey said. "Someone cracked him over the head and knocked him out, first, and then they let his head dangle in some water. They could have stuck him head first into the ocean, or they could have held him over a puddle, as far as that goes. The point of the matter is, he didn't drown by himself an' then get into the front seat of that Welcome Wagon. He was drowned, an' he got put there. That part of the figurin' is simple, doc—"

"Oh, it is, is it?" Cummings said. "I see. What you mean is, someone murdered Abner Grove. Yes. Quite so. But where?"

"Your guess," Asey told him, "is as good as mine. He might have been drowned there on the bog, or it might have happened fifty miles away—"

"Nonsense," Cummings said promptly. "If he was drowned somewhere else, why would someone stick him in that wagon and drive him over there to the bog?"

Asey got up from the table and walked over to the window.

"It wouldn't have been such a bad idea," he said. "It would have been a pretty bright idea. They hit him over the head, they drown him, they put him in Banbury's Welcome Wagon and they drive him in the wagon to Banbury's Bog, as close as they can get him to Banbury's house, without being seen—well, you get the idea. It throws a little more limelight on the spot that Banbury's already in—"

"Now, see here!" Cummings said. "You're not standing there and insinuating that someone's trying to involve Banbury in Grove's death!"

"They already have," Asey said gently. "They've already stuck Grove in Banbury's wagon, on Banbury's land, and—"

"What does that mean?" Cummings demanded. "They might have stuck him in your car or my car, and driven him to your front yard, or mine. But that wouldn't involve us, would it?"

"No," Asey said, "I don't know's it would, in a way, except that we'd get asked a lot of questions. With Banbury, it's different. Yesterday they called him a fine man. Last night they called him a poisoner. There's no reason why they can't go a step further today and call him a murderer."

Cummings snorted.

"That's the most ridiculous thing I ever listened to in my life, Asey! Listen, I like this man Banbury. I wouldn't believe him involved even if he had a motive for killing Grove. I wouldn't believe it even if he had the opportunity. Even if someone saw him stuffing Grove's head into a bucket of water! How can Banbury be involved!"

"The tide," Asey said, "was high around eleven last night—"

"My God, what's that got to do with it?"

"Wa-el," Asey drawled, "it's got quite a lot. It means that the Welcome Wagon got driven along by the bog before eleven o'clock last night. Then the tide come in, and washed away all the marks of feet, or tramplin' around. The ground was still squidgy and damp when Banbury and I came. If someone killed Grove there, by the bog, the tide's washed away all the marks and clews there might have been. If someone drove him there, and then left, all traces of them has got washed away. And I noticed last night that the steering wheel was sort of shinin' an' bright. If there was any fingerprints, you can bet they've been taken care of."

"Grove must have been drowned right there at the bog," Cummings said. "He must have. Think of the chances anyone would take otherwise, driving his body there. That white truck is conspicuous enough, anyone would see it and notice it."

"Why?" Asey said. "There's nothin' unusual in the sight of that vehicle whizzin' around. People is used to it. Grove could have been put on the floor, and somebody else have driven, without causin' any comment. Besides, with all the back roads over that way, you could get to that bog without goin' near the main road. The point, doc, is this. No one seen Abner after eight o'clock last night. I asked a lot of questions after I left you—lord knows every man-jack was up, last night, either bein' sick, or lookin' after someone who was. Nobody I talked with had seen Grove after eight o'clock. But everyone I spoke with told me that Banbury had been huntin' Grove, after the supper, and they all said he was boilin' mad and itchin' to get his fingers on Grove."

"I can understand that part," Cummings said. "Under the circumstances, if the tarts you'd made had turned out to be dusted with arsenic, you'd go to the selectmen, wouldn't you? And wouldn't even you be just a little sore?"

"Probably," Asey said, "but think this out, doc. I got to the Bog House around ten-thirty. Banbury had been huntin' Grove for an hour or so, by himself. You see what I mean?"

"You mean," Cummings said, "that if someone takes it into his head to accuse Banbury of killing Grove, Banbury hasn't any alibi, because Banbury was reputedly tearing around hunting Grove, with fire in his eye. And if the

Welcome Wagon was driven to the Bog before high tide—
oh, I see. I see what you're aiming at. But Banbury hasn't
any motive, Asey. Suppose Banbury *was* mad, and suppose
he was hunting Grove—lord, if he wanted to vent his
wrath on the selectmen, he had three to choose from! Why
pick Grove? Banbury wouldn't have any motive for killing
Abner Grove!"

"It wouldn't seem so," Asey agreed. "But—"

"Don't tell me those fools—those dolts, those jackasses!
Don't tell me that the intelligentsia of Weesit has provided
Banbury with a motive!"

"Accordin' to my cousin Jennie," Asey said, "who stuck
her ear to the party line for me at six this mornin', Weesit
has a motive. Seems, doc, that Grove was kind of a Galahad."

Cummings spluttered into his coffee.

"Galahad? That watery-eyed, weak-jawed, vacillating
creature?"

"He wasn't quite that bad lookin'," Asey said. "But it
seems, this mornin', that Grove was the fellow who's been
standin' up to Banbury when Banbury tried to overstep
the bounds—"

"What bounds?" Cummings demanded.

"Just bounds. That's what Jennie told me. She didn't
specify what bounds. And it seems that yesterday, on their
way back from Boston, Grove and Banbury had what
amounted to a fist fight. Don't splutter so, doc, you'll choke
again. That's the story accordin' to the party line. Weesit
thinks that Banbury poisoned the tarts to kill Abner off—"

"What about the other hundred and ninety-nine?" Cummings asked. "Did they think he wanted to polish them off,
too? Oh, it's too ridiculous! I'm speechless! I never before
was so completely speechless!"

For several minutes, Dr. Cummings enlarged on his
speechless state.

"It's absurd, the whole business," he wound up. "Absurd, nonsensical, ridiculous, preposterous, and downright
silly. And if you let them arrest Banbury, Asey Mayo, I'll
come over here and throw stones at your windows. Why, I
never dreamed, when those state coppers began asking
questions of Banbury, that there was any possibility of anything like this! Did you?"

Asey hesitated.

"You did!" Cummings said. "I see. That's why you beat it, and went off delving around on your own. I see. But does Banbury suspect anything like this? Does he have any idea of what Weesit's saying?"

"Banbury's sharp," Asey said, "but I don't think he has any idea of how serious this might get to be. I thought I'd drop over there and sort of discuss the situation with him, after breakfast— Who finally took the case for the state police—Farley?"

"Yes, Farley," Cummings said. "Asey, I sometimes wonder why, because a man looks well on a rapidly moving motorcycle, the powers that be all seem to feel that that man is destined to be a detective? Farley was a good routine cop. He wasn't a bad sergeant. As a lieutenant, he does things to my digestive system. Yes, I see what you mean. Farley will chat with Weesit, and Banbury will get the headlines. Asey, are you going to take steps? I think you should—"

"I feel the way you do," Asey said, "about this fellow Banbury. I think he's done too much good to be handed any raw deals. I like him. If they should take him and —what's the matter, Jennie?"

Jennie, his buxom cousin by marriage, was hovering at the door.

"It's this girl," she said, "that just rode up to the back door on a bicycle and wants to see you. She looks like an awful tramp, with a knapsack and everything, but she says she's Jane Banbury."

"Ask her in," Asey said. "No, wait. I'll go. I sort of think, doc, that things have already started to commence to happen."

It took Asey a full minute to recognize the girl in dirty overalls and a grease-stained sweatshirt who stood beside a dilapidated bicycle at the back steps. He couldn't tell just what Jane had done to herself, but something about her mouth and eyes made her look like a completely different sort of girl from the one he had met the night before at Banbury Bog.

She grinned at him.

"Just lipstick," she said, "and eye shadow. Mother said I looked like something you could crack."

"Why?" Asey said. "Why the—er—disguise? And the bicycle?"

"Don't laugh at my bicycle," Jane said. "About the only thing I ever really learned at college was how to ride a bike, and I'm glad I had all those years of practice before I tackled this little model. This wasn't ever meant to be ridden. Someone made it to display in a glass case at ten cents a look. I can't think where dad ever got it. Or why."

"I can't think," Asey surveyed the bicycle critically, "why you ever rode it."

"Oh," Jane said, "this was the only method of transportation that the cops overlooked. You can see how they would. Er—are you going to ask me in? Because I do want to see you. I'm what plays call a bearer of tidings."

Asey opened the door.

"Come in," he said. "So the cops have already begun?"

"The cops," Jane followed him in to the dining room, "have invaded Banbury Bog, Asey. They've taken it over—what a simply swell elegant house this is, I love it! Yes, wherever you look at Banbury Bog, there's a cop. They just ooze from every nook and cranny. Mother found one in her shower. They took all the car keys, you see, and the biggest, most sinister cop is standing by the phone, looking truculent. But in a way they've been very thoughtful. They said we could walk on the west porch."

"How's your father?" Asey inquired. "Oh, this is Doc Cummings, or did you meet him in the shuffle last night? How's your father?"

"Dad and mother were washing the breakfast dishes when I left," Jane said, "under the watchful eye of a cop."

Cummings stared at her.

"Don't tell me they've set your family to work washing dishes!"

"Oh, no. It's just that the servants have left. En masse. They said they wouldn't stay in the same house with a dirty poisoner and murderer. So they left. I don't know whether they were the ones that broke the windows and sunk my boat, or if the local boys did that. Anyway, they left, and popsie got a chance to cook breakfast. He loves to cook. He and momsie always squabble over who's going to make the muffins—well, to sum it all up, we're more or less incommunicado, up at Banbury Bog, and momsie thought someone ought to talk with you, Asey, before they drag dad off to jail. So I came."

Cummings pounded the table with his fist.

"D'you mean to tell me, they're holding you there? Asey, can you beat it? They're really holding you?"

"Well," Jane said, "we weren't handcuffed, or anything, but they yelled at mother when she stepped off the porch to yank up a poor little weed, and we know they have the car keys, because they demanded 'em. And the man at the phone just didn't seem to hear when I asked if he'd let me make a call."

"How'd you get away?" Asey asked.

"I put on these clothes, and slipped down the back stairs and sort of slithered through the garden to the crowd —"

"So you've got a crowd, have you?"

Jane nodded. "A vast throng, all muttering and making sinister noises, and hurling an occasional stone. I joined up with them, and muttered, and made sinister noises, too, and threw a couple of stones, just to get into the spirit of the thing, and then I marched down to the boat house and got that awful bike. I'd never have got here if a truck driver hadn't given me a hitch. Somehow," Jane added meditatively, "I think he's going to be surprised when he finds out I've gone. The lipstick and the eye shadow went to his head. Asey, momsie wanted to know if you have any plans."

"I'd intended," Asey told her, "to go over and investigate this subversive propaganda about your father, and sort of break the news to him that something like this might just possibly come to pass."

Jane grinned.

"I think he guessed. I know that momsie did. And each of 'em tried to keep it from the other, to spare 'em. That's one of the favorite Banbury games, sparing each other bad news. It usually turns out that we all blurt it out at once, in unison. Well, Asey, momsie wanted to know about your plans, if you had any, and how about making some, if you didn't. They're in a terrible sweat."

"I can understand it," Asey said.

"Oh, about you. Not this mess. About you. They don't dare ask you to go on the Banbury payroll—that Porter roadster and the white flannels knocked 'em speechless. And they don't feel they know you well enough just to ask your help. They gave me a long, tactful speech to make you, but I've forgotten it, and besides, I knew you would help. So did they. And you will, won't you? Because dad's a pretty swell man, and this is a pretty lousy business."

Something, Asey noticed, was running in Jane's eye shadow, and her fingers, as she lighted a cigarette, were not entirely steady.

"Of course he will!" Cummings answered. "So will I. Asey, let's go give Farley the works, and put a stop to this damn foolishness—"

"But dad and momsie thought," Jane interrupted quickly, "that maybe it'd be better for Potface—I mean Farley, to arrest dad in a hurry, and repent at leisure. Isn't that your idea, too, Asey? Dad thought it would give you a freer hand, and take the cops away from our house. He's worrying about mother's blood pressure, you see. And she thinks it's a good idea, because she's frightened to death that dad'll lose his temper, and there's practically no telling what might happen then. When dad stops being philosophical, he's inclined to remember his first bakery, down on Avenue A, and he takes to his fists. And—did I bring in that knapsack? I see it. I've got two peachy clews for you to play with."

As she undid the straps, Jane felt Asey's blue eyes watching her, and the color rose in her cheeks.

"I know what you're thinking," she said, sitting back on her heels, "and it isn't true. If you want to know the truth, the Banbury family's scared to death. We all feel like something in a play. As momsie said, all they really needed was a snowstorm to drive us out into. It just doesn't seem real. It—oh, I don't know how to describe it. But if we stopped and thought, we'd go mad."

"I don't see how you've managed to stay sane this long," Cummings said. "My God, it's too unbelievable! It's all based on such vague, intangible things!"

"There's nothing vague and intangible about that crowd on the edge of the bog," Jane said. "Nor the stones they throw. You know, to be greeted in the early morning by a fusillade of stones through the windows is new to the Banburys. Even when dad had the strikes, no one threw any stones. Why, they even took time off the strike to bake dad a birthday cake! Look, Asey, I brought one of the stones over for you. Here. With note."

Asey snapped off the elastic band that held the crumpled piece of paper on the stone Jane took from the knapsack.

He whistled as he read the straggling capitals, and Cummings, reading over his shoulder, launched into a fresh dissertation on his state of complete and utter speechlessness about the whole situation.

"What do they mean by it!" he said. "What do they *mean* by it? 'Keep Asey Mayo out of this!' For the love of God, do they think a thing like that would keep you away?"

"No," Asey said, "I think they hope to get me in. My, my. This gets sort of interestin'. I'm beginnin' to take a personal interest in this. Somebody's awful sure of themselves, doc. They're so sure, they're knockin' the chip off for me. What else you got, Jane?"

"Well," Jane said, "first I ought to explain. Two or three nights this week, when I've come home, I've caught sight of someone flitting about the house, outdoors. But I didn't think anything about it, because maids always flit about. And ours just know everyone, and they have a constant stream of visitors. But night before last, after Evan Chase and I decided that something was wrong, he and I sort of flitted after this woman. She flitted first, though, and we didn't get anywhere. But on my way into the house, after I'd said good-night to him, I found this—isn't it silly? Stones thrown through windows, with notes. And pins turning up on the flagstones after strange women have flitted around. It's so damn silly! If I heard it over the radio, I'd turn it off. If I saw it in the movies, I'd howl. But it happens. Here, here's the pin. It may or may not mean a thing. I didn't even bother to show it to momsie—"

Jane broke off her monologue rather abruptly.

She knew perfectly well who the pin belonged to, and she was entirely sure that it had been dropped by the person flitting around. It hadn't been dropped by any casual visitor, because casual visitors didn't use that door, or that path. They came by the front door.

But, as a matter of policy, she didn't intend to name the owner of the pin. Her family would never believe her, and she didn't think that even Asey Mayo would believe her. Her family would say that there were thousands of blue enamel pins in the world, and Asey would probably agree.

Asey turned the pin over in his hand.

"It's a droppable thing," he said. "No safety clasp. Any idea who it might belong to, Jane?"

Jennie Mayo, entering the dining room with a tray, spared Jane the necessity of making some sort of answer.

"I know who it belongs to," she said. "I've seen that pin a million times. Has it got a little nick in one corner? I thought so. That pin belongs to Cousin Tabitha Sparrow, Asey. Uncle Fred's wife left it to her."

CHAPTER IV

Asey looked from Jennie to the little blue enamel pin in his hand.

Then, quizzically, he looked at Jane.

The girl's poker face, he thought, was like her father's, but nowhere near as expert. She had known that it was Tabitha's pin, all the time.

"Oh, if it's Tabitha's," Jane said easily, "that just lets the pin out as a clew, doesn't it? She never could have been the woman flitting about, of course! It never could have been Tabitha. Mother says she's the one person we can rely on through anything. She's been simply marvelous to us ever since we came."

Jennie nodded sagely.

"Tabitha thinks you're the finest folks she ever knew," she said. "She just can't say enough good things about you, and what your father's done. She thinks your father's a mighty fine man."

"Yes," Jane said, extinguishing a cigarette with elaborate care, "yes, she likes father."

"Your father, he looks sort of like her husband," Jennie said. "Remember Duncan Sparrow, Asey? Don't you think Mr. Banbury's like him? I mean, in looks. Duncan was a big man. Poor Tabitha, I don't know whether to feel sorry for her or not. About Abner Grove, I mean. Folks kept saying that those two intended to marry, and I suppose if Tabitha liked him, that was all right. But just the samey, I always thought he was a kind of a wishy-washy man."

"Hemmy-and-hawey," Jane suggested.

"That's just it! And Tabitha's got more brains in her little finger than Abner Grove ever had in his whole head. Somehow, it never seemed to me they'd ever make a go of it. But Tabitha certainly thinks a lot of your father."

"Uh-huh," Jane said. "Well, Asey, Tabitha's been around the house a lot, and I suppose she just lost that pin one day, and I suppose I just happened to find it the other night. I'm sure there's not the slightest connection between my finding the pin then, and the person flitting about. Er—will you give the pin back to her, Asey, or shall I?"

Asey, who was looking out of the window, didn't appear to hear her question.

"Jennie," he said "whisk those dishes off the table. We got some more comp'ny."

Dr. Cummings got up and peered curiously over his shoulder at the sedan which had just drawn up in front of the house.

"Who, the cops? Oh! Tabitha, and Judge Chase—isn't he a pompous old geezer! Who's that other woman, Marian Milton? Asey, this looks to me like a delegation."

Asey grinned.

"I think it is," he said, as he turned away from the window. "They got a kind of purposeful air about 'em."

He paused and looked at Jane, who was lighting another cigarette. A little smile was playing around her lips, and she flicked her match into the fireplace with a jaunty snap of her fingers. She obviously felt pleased with herself, and Asey knew why. Her deft insinuations about Tabitha Sparrow's feeling for Phineas Banbury would have done credit to many an older and more experienced woman.

"Jennie," Asey said, "I wish you'd go out and chat with those people an' stall 'em for a few minutes, will you? I want to get somethin' settled before they come bargin' in. Thanks. Say, doc, when was Grove killed? What time?"

Cummings shrugged.

"Around nine or ten. You can't really tell, Asey. Might have been earlier or later. You can sort of set the limits yourself. If you think the Welcome Wagon was driven down by the bog before eleven and before the high tide, then he was killed before eleven. If people saw him around eight, then you know he was alive then. Crandall might be able to tell you more later, but I doubt it."

"I thought," Jane said, "that watches always stopped when people were killed. They always do in books, the minute someone gets shot."

Cummings pointed out that Abner Grove wasn't shot.

"Besides," he said, "Abner didn't have a watch."

"He certainly did!" Jane said. "Father presented all the selectmen with watches, the day they had the grand opening and dedication of the Whaling Museum. Engraved with all sorts of fine and lofty sentiments, too. I made a special trip to Boston to see they were done properly. Why, Bearse and Grove and Baldy were so proud, they went around asking the time of everyone they met, just so they could have an excuse to pull out their new watches. Momsie and I thought of throwing in some gold chains, so they could wear the watches around their necks. Of course Abner Grove had a watch! If he didn't have it in his pocket last night, it'll be the first time he ever left it home since he got given it!"

"Well, he must have," Cummings said. "He didn't have a watch on him last night. Asey, is there anything you'd like me to do?"

"You might drop over and chat with Farley. But," he added earnestly, "don't go flyin' off the handle, doc, an' gettin' him all riled up. See if they had the fingerprint lads down, an' what the experts have come to the conclusion that. Jane, would you take it hard if I asked you to go read a magazine out in the kitchen with Jennie? She'll probably feed you some fresh gingerbread, if you act real nice. You see, it's just possible that this delegation'll speak more free an' open if you're not here."

But Asey called Jane back as she and Dr. Cummings left.

"Tell me, how long have you been raisin' your eyebrows over Cousin Tab?"

Jane became the picture of appalled innocence.

"What? Why, Asey Mayo! What do you mean! Tabitha's the best friend the Banburys have in all Weesit. Momsie's devoted to her. She, and Judge Chase and Marian Milton have all helped dad—"

"Ever since you came," Asey inquired, "or has it only shown up lately?"

Jane refused to be cornered.

"Really, Asey," she said, "I'm afraid I must have given you the wrong impression entirely. You know dad. He's one of those large, massive, comfortable men that women like. The fact that he's utterly devoted to momsie doesn't keep other women from—well, liking him. I said that your cousin Tabitha liked him, and so she does. So does Marian Milton. They just think he's a peachy man, that's all, and if you choose to put any other interpretations on it, you've got a nasty mind."

"Go along with you," Asey said, "and eat gingerbread, and if you was a few years younger, I'd turn you over and whack you."

"Your own cousin!" Jane said. "And you make such suggestions. Your own cousin!"

"She's not my own cousin," Asey returned. "She's about a sixth cousin a few times removed. Huh. Was that what's been holdin' you back, that cousin business?"

"If you want to know, yes. Among other items, like the family's liking her a lot, and trusting her implicitly—yes, I'm coming, doctor!"

Asey frowned as he went through the other door and out to the front yard, where he rescued Tabitha and Judge Chase and Marian Milton from Jennie's tireless tongue.

He ushered the trio, with a certain amount of formality, into his parlor.

They were all nervous, he noticed, and they rather dawdled over the process of taking off their coats and getting themselves settled. Judge Chase adjusted his black tie and wing collar several times, although it looked perfectly all right to Asey. Tabitha kept clearing her throat, and fussing with the buckle on the belt of her dark print dress. Mrs. Milton removed the bandanna she had tied around her hair, and stuffed it into the pocket of her tweed coat. Then she pulled it out and put it back on her head. Someone out in the hall, Asey thought, might have guessed that the three of them were suffering from severe head colds, the way they all kept blowing their noses.

Tabitha finally stopped clearing her throat and came to the point.

"Asey," she said, "I'm sure you know why we're here. Asey, d'you know they've been insane enough to arrest Phineas Banbury?"

"Already?" Asey said, in surprise. "Farley either's jumped to a whale of a lot of conclusions, or else he must have been uncommon brisk in his detectin'."

"It was that beastly arsenic!" Tabitha said. "They found it in the cellar at Banbury Bog. Phineas told them the truth, that the arsenic was there when he bought the house, and as far as he knew, the Phillipses were responsible for it. Farley asked him why he left it there, and Phineas said they used it to get rid of the rats. The old barn was simply overrun with rats, you know. He finally had to have an exterminator come from Boston. But Farley just brushed all that aside, and arrested him for poisoning those tarts."

"Oho," Asey said. "For that. Not for the murder?"

The trio before him seemed to freeze at the word murder.

"I thought," Asey went on, "they might try and pin that on him."

"Well," Marian Milton said, "we think so too. That's why we've come here, Asey. We want you to take—"

"Steps," Judge Chase finished her sentence for her. "I told Banbury that I would be happy to call a few friends and have Farley put in his place, but he said no, he didn't mind being arrested, and at least it would stop his wife from being pestered by the police. He doesn't seem to mind what happens to him, as long as she isn't worked up. He asked me to see you, at once. Now, Asey, I want to go into this whole situation very thoroughly with you. We all do—"

The Judge talked on, and on, endlessly, Asey thought. And he didn't add much to the information Asey already had. All three of them had felt the difference in the attitude of the town toward Banbury, and all were convinced that someone who was responsible for the propaganda was also responsible for the arsenic put in the tarts.

"But," Tabitha interrupted the Judge's monologue, "they wouldn't necessarily have used that arsenic of Banbury's, would they, Asey? Any arsenic would have done. And it would have been a simple matter, I suppose, for someone to have got the arsenic into the tarts. Phineas and Lu made them, and left the bakery when they were done. Mawson, the regular baker, tends to the store, too, and while he waited on customers out in front, anyone could have slipped in back and scattered that arsenic around. Why, when I was there yesterday morning to get frankfurt rolls for the Abbotts' grandchildren's weenie roast, I thought then how easy it would be for someone to slip in and steal some. I could see the tarts, cooling in the racks. But I never thought of anything worse happening than their being stolen."

"It needn't have happened in the bakery," Mrs. Milton said. "It could have happened later. Mawson put the racks in the Welcome Wagon before he left for the day, and I saw him lock the wagon up. I'd just taken his wife over— she works for me now. But a car door lock doesn't mean so much. I've picked my own with a hairpin, and I'm sure a lock wouldn't stand in the way of someone who intended to poison those tarts—"

"As a matter of fact," Judge Chase broke in, "the poison would have been administered to the tarts even after Grove took the wagon. He was driving it, you know, Asey, while the regular man's away. Now, it so happens that Grove stopped by at my house en route to the East Weesit church with the tarts, and he left both the wagon and the pastry outside my house for at least fifteen minutes. I had been looking into the title of a wood lot for him, and he very much desired to have some information on it by last night. But the point I wish to make is this, that the wagon and the pastry were left outside my home, unguarded, so to speak, for some time. And, furthermore—"

"I'd say," Asey made a valiant effort to wrest the conversation from the Judge before he got too rhetorical, "that the world was sort of fraught with op'tunities for an enterprisin' man who wanted to poison them tarts. Er —is there anythin' more you folks had in mind to tell me?"

He hoped, quite fervently, that there was not. He was weary of talk. He wanted to get Jane, and get over to Weesit, and start doing things.

"Well," Mrs. Milton said hesitantly, "yes. Will you tell him, Tabitha, or shall I? About the stones?"

"Oho, more stones?" Asey asked. "As, stones thrown at you?"

Tabitha shook her head. "Stones on our respective doorsteps, this morning. Sitting there, holding down notes. Here, here's mine. Got yours, Marian? Where's yours, Judge?"

Asey spread the three pieces of paper out on the table. They were about the same size, and the same message was printed, in pencil, on all three.

" 'You helped Banbury,' " he read the single sentence aloud, " 'Beware.' "

"What do you think of that?" Tabitha demanded.

"It's crisp an' to the point, ain't it?" Asey said. "You helped Banbury, an' you better watch out. No beatin' about the bush. Just pure, unadultered fact. You helped him an' was nice to him, so they got it in for you, too."

He thought he began to understand why his visitors had been nervous. Personally, he enjoyed a good, challenging threat. It acted as a stimulus. But then, he had received a good many threats in his life, and these people hadn't. Very likely they were scared stiff by those notes. At any rate, they had probably thought twice before coming to ask his aid.

"What you goin' to do about these messages?" he asked.

"Well," Mrs. Milton said, "I think we all feel the same way about it. I think we're all a little afraid. I know that I am. No matter how much you rationalize and tell yourself that if anything really awful were going to happen, someone would do it without bothering to write little notes, nevertheless, there's a warning. On the other hand, Asey, Phineas Banbury has done more for me than anyone in this world ever did. For five years I've tried to work my rug business up into something you could call a business, and now, thanks to him, it is. I can't tell you how many things he's done for me. Why, he's even lent me a car when mine smashed up! I don't just know what I can do, but I want to help him out of this mess. And I'm going to, no matter how many warning notes get left on my doorstep!"

"So am I, Asey!" Tabitha said. "And for the same reason."

Judge Chase nodded.

"As you may know, Asey," he said, "I've compiled several volumes on the history of Weesit since I retired and came home to live, and I can truthfully say that not since the days of my grandfather, the late great judge, has there been such enterprise and such prosperity in the town. Phineas Banbury alone is responsible for it. Without any thought of personal gain, or any effort to take credit, he has put Weesit back into the place she once held. I should have been proud to have done, myself, one-tenth of what he has accomplished. I love my town. For that reason alone, even if I did not like Phineas Banbury and admire him personally, I should come here and ask your aid. There is no threat that means more to me than my town."

Tabitha got up.

"I can only say 'Amen' to that. Asey, you'll do what you can, won't you? And call on us for anything at all."

"Sure, I'll do what I can," Asey put his hand into his pocket. "An', before I forget it, I've got a pin belongs to you. Jennie said this was yours."

"Now that relieves me!" Judge Chase said. "That's the one you thought you lost at my house the other morning, isn't it, Tabitha? Evan and I hunted and hunted for it. Asey, any time Banbury wants to be released, let me know, and I'll start phoning. I think I still know enough influential people."

Asey smiled. Judge Chase, he knew, could spend ten minutes at a telephone and have half the Republican party ready to go to bat.

When he returned from seeing them to their car, Asey found Jane in the hall.

"I thought they'd never go," she said. "Asey, isn't the Judge a dear old thing? Sometimes he's exasperating, he runs on so, but doesn't he love his town!"

"Why not?" Asey said. "There've been Chases in Weesit for over three hundred years. Sure he loves the town. He's a real Cape Codder. He went away to work, but he came home to die."

"What a strange way to put it," Jane said. "But they do come back, don't they? There are a lot of elderly, retired people who've come back to town to live. I suppose, in a way, that's why we're here, really— Asey, what did Tabitha say when you gave her back the pin? I couldn't hear."

"No good," Asey informed her with mock severity, "ever come from eavesdroppin'."

Jane grinned.

"That's just what Jennie said you'd say. Her ear was glued beside mine—"

"No, it wasn't," Jennie retorted, as she entered the room. "Don't you believe her, Asey. She forced me to leave my work an' come listen. Asey, wasn't it funny that Tabitha never said a single thing about Abner Grove? None of 'em did. They didn't say a word about his bein' killed. Tabitha didn't even look red around the eyes. Why, they didn't even say they felt bad about Abner!"

"They probably would of," Asey said, "if I'd give 'em a chance, an' hadn't hustled 'em off. Jane, I want to get started. You—"

"But is *is* queer," Jane said. "Both Tabitha and Marian Milton seemed a lot more upset about dad, didn't they? In fact, Jennie and I thought they were going to burst into tears over him, at one point. Marian's just a little soft about dad, too."

"I noticed that," Jennie said. "That tweedy kind of woman sort of clings, don't they, when you come right down to it?"

"Jennie," Jane said, "you and momsie are soul mates. I've got to bring you two together, and let you go through the female population. Momsie says Marian is a scheming thing, and she was furious when dad lent Marian her sedan. I caught her muttering something about women who wore neckties—"

"Speakin' of neckties," Jennie interrupted, "you go change your shirt, Asey, if you're goin' off detectin'. An' put on a necktie, for gracious sakes! It's terrible, Jane, the way that man dresses. You'd never think he had a closet full of nice clothes upstairs, made by Bill Porter's own tailor. An' will he ever wear 'em? No. Those ole pants, an' that ole flannel shirt— Asey, will you go change?"

"No," Asey said, "I won't. I got too much of my time taken up this mornin' to bother wastin' more on sartorial d'tails, Jennie. You lay out some clothes, an' when I come home, I'll dress up for you."

It never entered his head, when he left the house with Jane, that he wouldn't enter it again for two days.

"This car!" Jane said. "What a thing! Asey, before I die, can I drive this car? All my life I've wanted to drive a Porter sixteen."

"You like it?" Asey said. "You—no, that's the rear, Jane. This is the front. You'd ought to have seen Betsey Porter when Bill brought this new model around for her to see. She took one look, an' then she shook her head an' went off to Boston for a week, an' when she come back, she had an ole Model Fifty-five, built in nineteen-fifteen. She's driven it ever since, all summer."

"Why?" Jane demanded.

"As a protest." Asey chuckled. "Betsey claims that when she gets into a car, she don't want to have to stop an' think which direction she was goin' when she parked it, so as to know which way she's headed then. Myself, I think Bill's engineers kind of jumped the gun as far as the looks is concerned, but the engine's a corker. Jane, shall we go back to your house an' reassure your mother that we're all right, an' that we've got your father on our minds, an' have Farley order you to stay put there, or shall we set to work?"

"To work," Jane said. "No, I guess you'd better let me go back to momsie. Oddly enough, I'm sure she's going to feel better with dad arrested than with him loose, because she'll feel he's out of danger. She has a feeling that dad's in great personal danger."

"I can understand that," Asey said.

"And, of course, there's less chance of his losing his temper and flying off the handle. I mean, to the extent of his doing real damage. But just the same, I ought to go see her. Maybe you can tell us where you'll be, and we can find you, or meet you, or something like that."

"Right." Asey started the car. "All ready?"

Jane didn't understand what he meant by that question until the car started down the straightaway beyond Asey's house.

When they branched off, at the same breath-taking speed, on a curving dirt road, Jane reached forward and unashamedly gripped the dash with both hands.

"Is this," she asked respectfully, "your usual speed? Do you always clip along at this pace, Asey?"

Asey grinned, without taking his eyes from the rutted road ahead.

"Oh, no," he said. "This is sort of a fancy model, an' I got another shift before she really starts rollin'. Some day I'll take you to Bill's track an' put her in high."

They reached Weesit without going near any tarred road, a fact which amazed Jane.

"I'm sort of fond of the lanes," Asey said, slowing down. "There's a lot of 'em, an' you don't get hung up with a lot of tourists, zig-zaggin' along at twenty-five so as not to miss any of the beauties of quaint Cape Cod. Jane, I'm goin' to let you off in the village, an' let you get home by yourself. For my own fell reasons, I don't want to see Farley yet."

"Won't he like your being on our side?"

"Wa-el," Asey said, "to be honest with you, I don't think he will, much. An' I think that if Farley gets given enough rope, he'll hang himself, an' it's just possible he might pick up a few restrainin' thoughts from me. Jane, if you or your mother wants me, I'm goin' to be at Abner Grove's house, over on the meadow. I'll be there for an hour or more."

"If you leave before we get to you," Jane said, "leave a note. Blaze a tree, or something."

"I'll leave a trail of beans— Jane, if you'll get out here at this path, an' walk at a reasonable rate, you'd ought to be home in less'n ten minutes."

"How you know this place!" Jane said, as she got out of the car. "I never thought, but that's the lane around the bog, isn't it?" She paused. "Asey, there's something sticking out of your back tire, did you know it? Come look."

Asey got out and surveyed the nail tip which protruded from the white side wall.

"That's what you get," Jane said, "from driving over your lanes."

"No," Asey said, "it's what I get for not lookin' at my tires before I set out. On back lanes, you pick up old rusty nails, an' you get a puncture. This is a nice, new, shiny nail."

He got a pair of pliers from a pocket in the car, and proceeded to pull the nice, shiny nail out.

"See?" he said. "Someone stuck it in, but they didn't have time to make a good, thorough job of it, so when we got goin', the nail just skewered through the tread. Huh."

"I'm thinking," Jane said, "of the speed and celerity with which we covered those lanes, Asey. Suppose that nail had gone into the tire!"

"Then," Asey returned coolly, "the fellow who wants me kept out of this would be all happy an' satisfied, wouldn't he? Well, well. I'll be more careful after this. I didn't hardly think there'd been time enough to start any sabotage on my car, yet."

"Used to it, are you?"

Asey sighed. "My, yes! 'Course, it is the quickest way to get rid of me, doin' somethin' to my car. But it gets sort of tiresome. I sh'd think people'd give it up as a bad job. You'd think this fellow'd have enough sense to know that there wouldn't be anything he could do to my car that'd turn out to be serious, without my knowin' it."

"Perhaps," Jane said, "it wasn't a fellow."

"Women," Asey informed her, "don't usually tamper with cars. They don't know enough about 'em to try. If they do know anything, they play with the steerin' gear— Jane, you trot along. I'll see you later."

He watched Jane as she set out on the footpath, waved as she turned out of sight, and then sat for a moment with his arms resting on the steering wheel.

After several minutes' thought, he turned the car around and embarked on a series of short cuts and side roads. There was a very direct road to Abner Grove's house, and he knew it.

"But," he murmured, "I just think I'll sneak up on the place, for fun."

Parking the car in a pine grove on a hill above Grove's meadow, Asey started slowly down toward the little half house.

He tried to think, as he went along, why on earth anyone should kill Abner Grove.

The poisoned tarts, the difference in the attitude of people toward Banbury were all clear enough, in their way. Somebody, Asey thought, was trying to knock Phineas Banbury off the pedestal he'd achieved more or less in spite of himself.

But you could hardly go so far as to claim that someone had killed Abner Grove just to add to all that, or to annoy Banbury, or involve him.

Asey paused to light his pipe.

Grove was a sincere and honest sort of man, but he was vacillating. Everyone had brought that up. Grove's most notable characteristic was an inability to make up his mind. He was no Don Juan, so there was no need to enter into the triangle angle, or to hunt around for jealous husbands or thwarted lady-lovers. Certainly Grove didn't have enough money for anyone to bother killing him for. He had a large mortgage, Asey knew, because Grove's lack of interest in making payments had been brought up and thoroughly discussed at the last bank meeting which he, himself, had attended in the role of director. Grove hadn't been killed with any motive of immediate robbery, because there had been money in the wallet that was in his pocket.

That, Asey thought, didn't get him anywhere, but at least he was narrowing things down. Grove knew of the changed attitude toward Banbury. Mrs. Banbury had been positive on that point. It was possible that Grove had even known the identity of the person responsible.

Asey sat down on a convenient stump, and dallied with that thought.

Suppose that Grove, after the effects of the poisoned tarts began to be felt, had sought out that person. Suppose Grove had talked, and remonstrated with the person. Suppose he had made threats of what he would do if the person did not at once confess to his crime.

That, Asey decided, would do it.

Grove wouldn't have either the courage or the sense to tell anyone else first. That would require making a decision, and Grove probably would have avoided it. He would have gone to the person he thought was guilty, and hemmed, and hawed, and talked, and remonstrated, and then finally threatened.

Then, probably, the person had cracked Grove over the head.

"Now," he said to himself, "we're gettin' somewhere, Mayo. You crack Grove over the head. He's got you sore. He falls over, kerplunk, and what do you do? Now, suppose you leave him— Aha. You leave him. You're getting scared, now. You beat it. Then you come back, and— Yes, sir, I think that's it. You find that his head landed in a puddle, or in water somewhere, an' Grove is dead. An' as you stand there, shakin' an' quakin', it occurs to you that this's the place where you got your chance to give Banbury the works. Huh. Now, I wonder why that should occur to you? I don't know's it would occur to me."

He puffed away at his pipe and then he nodded.

"Oho. I get it. In the interval of hittin' Grove an' returnin' to find him dead, you've had time an' op'tunity to find out that Banbury's been tearin' around huntin' Grove like a Comanche on the warpath. So, you put Grove into the wagon, an' you take him to Banbury's Bog. Because you can leave him there, an' be sure that the incomin' tide'll take care of your footprints, an' besides, you can slip away on foot, without bein' seen. All you got to do is just leave

Grove there, an' let time take its course. Banbury's the fellow that'll get asked the questions an' have to make explanations—"

He got up suddenly from the stump, and stared down at Grove's house, just beneath him on the meadow.

A woman had appeared around the corner of the house.

After a furtive look around, she raised her hand, and threw into the bushes something that glittered in the sun.

Then, almost at once, she seemed to regret the action, and started running in the direction the glittering object had taken.

Asey's eyes narrowed.

Doubtless she had some adequate explanation, but, on the whole, he thought this seemed a little queer on the part of his Cousin Tabitha.

CHAPTER V

Asey CONTINUED TO WATCH
from the hill as Tabitha parted the bushes and searched
frantically for whatever it was that she had thrown away.
Having carefully marked the spot where the object fell,
Asey was in a position to know that she had the wrong line
entirely. The thing that glittered had caromed off a good
twenty feet to the right.

The longer she hunted, the more obviously upset Tabitha became. She was down on her hands and knees, now,
groping and prodding. And, every now and then, she
turned her head and listened, or walked back to the corner
of the house and looked. But not once did she raise her
eyes toward the spot where Asey stood above her.

He let ten minutes slip by before he started casually to
stroll down the slope.

The sound of his shoes scraping against some dry twigs
sent Tabitha jumping to her feet.

For a moment she stood there, watching him approach.
And, Asey thought, if ever he saw a woman petrified with
fear, that woman was his Cousin Tabitha Sparrow.

As he passed by the spot where the object had fallen,
Asey bent over, and picked it up.

It was, he discovered, the gold knob of a cane that had
been sawed off about an inch below the knob.

Pausing, Asey read the inscription engraved on it.

"Presented to Phineas Banbury, Esq., by the Selectmen
and the Board of Trade of Weesit."

She had sawed that knob off herself, Asey thought,

and not very long ago, because there was still sawdust on the end. And that was the way women always sawed things, slantingly and sort of ridged, making things look as though someone had chewed on them.

Putting the knob into his pocket, Asey walked over to her.

"Tabitha," he said, "just what's your general purpose here?"

Tabitha looked at him, and her lips began to quiver. In another second, she had burst into a torrent of tears.

Asey waited for her to get over it. He never ceased to be amazed at the way women reacted to things. Here was Tabitha, who'd worked hard for her living ever since Duncan Sparrow died. Before he died, too, as far as that went. Tabitha had probably, in the course of her life, met up with any number of misfortunes and catastrophes and emergencies, and faced them by herself. But here she was, weeping away uncontrollably. On the other hand, there was Mrs. Banbury last night. There she and her husband were, in the position of being accused of poisoning a couple of hundred people, and Mrs. Banbury had gone at the matter of giving him details with a brisk and dry-eyed efficiency. Little Mrs. Banbury had probably always been protected and kept from unpleasant situations. But Tabitha was the one who broke down.

"Oh, Asey!" Tabitha said miserably, "I had to! I simply had to get rid of it, don't you see? I had to get rid of it! It was lying right there, beside the old cistern—don't you see, Asey, that cane is what someone used to hit Abner with! And they left it there beside the cistern, and those tubs with the water—oh, don't you see, Asey? If the police found that cane of his, Phineas wouldn't have a chance! And they couldn't have helped finding it. It was right there for them to find!"

Asey looked at her curiously.

He was not surprised that her reasoning as to the method of Abner's death paralleled his own. Tabitha was shrewd enough to figure things out, and there was probably no one in town who did not know that Abner had a lump on his head, and a stained, wet collar and tie, that he had been struck, and then drowned.

But Asey was surprised at the means she took to get rid

of what she considered damaging evidence, and he said as much.

"What on earth would you do a thing like that for?" he repeated. "Going to all the work of sawin' off the head of a cane, an' throwin' the knob into a mess of beach plum bushes, an' then scavengin' around after it! Honest to goodness. Tab, that don't hold water."

Tabitha wiped her eyes.

"I don't know why I did it, Asey. I guess I was just in a panic. I knew it was silly the minute I threw it. I knew it was a silly thing to do when I sawed it off. Asey, have you been watching me? I know you have. And that pin —where did you find that pin? I thought I lost it at the Judge's the other morning. That clasp is so bad. I've wanted to get a new one for a long while, and it's one of the things I was going to have done when I went to Boston this fall. Where did you find that pin?"

"Jane found it," Asey watched her closely. "Outside Bog House. She found it after she'd been investigatin' some woman that was flittin' around the other night."

"Good Lord!" Tabitha said in horror. "No wonder that girl has been eyeing me lately! Oh, Asey, how perfectly awful! Someone must have found it when I lost it the other day—anyone who knows me would recognize that pin! And they left it around—oh, how perfectly awful! And there I was at the bakery, yesterday! Oh, Asey! And now you find me doing this ridiculous thing! Oh!"

Asey agreed that there was a certain degree of awkwardness in her position.

"What'll I do?" Tabitha said. "Why, there's more—what do you call it? Circumstantial evidence? Well, there's certainly more of it hanging around me than around Phineas Banbury! What'll I do, Asey?"

"Well," Asey said, "you might produce a cast iron alibi, Tab, placin' you somewhere, with somebody reliable, from eight until eleven o'clock last night."

"Is that all?" Tabitha said. "That's easy. From quarter to eight until eleven-thirty, I played cribbage with Mr. Abbott. I loathe cribbage, and with all that excitement going on last night, cribbage was the last thing I wanted to play. But I played it, and I'm happy to tell you that the Abbotts have reserved their rooms for all of next summer. Oh, I can't tell you how relieved I am, Asey!"

"So," Asey said drily, "am I. Tab, what's this cane knob mean? You're sure it's Banbury's cane?"

Tabitha explained that at the dedication of the Whaling Museum, Phineas had presented watches to the selectmen.

"They got wind of the fact that something was coming," she said, "and in a burst of good feeling, they presented Phineas with a cane—"

"A cane! For the love of all that's sensible an' reasonable, Tab, why'd they give him a cane? A cane!"

Tabitha smiled.

"I understand from Abner, they asked Judge Chase what would be a good thing to give Phineas, and the Judge said a cane was always nice. He told them that the presentation of a neat, dignified cane was an old Weesit tradition. They gave one to Aspinet, the Indian chief, after—"

"After snatchin' the town away from him?"

"Exactly. And they gave a cane to General Grant, when he opened the railroad as far as Weesit— Well, the Judge told them a cane would be eminently suitable."

Asey rocked with laughter.

"A cane," he said, "is just about as em'nently suitable for that man as roller skates would be for a cod fish. Oh, my! That tickles me. Tab, someone's scattered your pin around for someone else to find, an' someone's left Banbury's cane here to be found. Now, there's no problem in guessin' that you can sum that someone up as an enemy you an' Banbury sort of got in common. Who could it be?"

Tabitha thought for a moment.

"I don't think I've got any enemies, Asey. Of course, there's always a certain percentage of people you know who don't like you much. But I can't think of any enemies. I don't see how I could have made any. I've just gone along, minding my own business, and trying to get the taxes paid."

"What about Abner?" Asey asked. "I don't like to go proddin' into personal things, but they told me you sort of went around with him."

She hesitated before replying.

"I don't quite know how to explain that," she said. "Weesit— Well, it's a small town, and people talk. I'm fond of the women in Weesit, but their interests are limited. Once in a while I find the masculine point of view refreshing.

And if I went to the movies, or chatted for any length of time with the husbands of the women I know, the results would have been terrific. Abner was unattached, and though he wasn't brilliant, he was well read, and he was away from the town enough when he was young to have something to talk about aside from Weesit. That's all there is to that."

"I see," Asey said. "But was there— Is there any other woman in town that might have sort of coveted Abner, as you might say? Perhaps that Mrs. Milton?"

Tabitha laughed aloud.

"Marian can't— I mean, she couldn't stand him. She thought he was weak. And he couldn't bear her. She nearly drove him frantic, in the days before Phineas came, bringing Abner all the little problems she thought he ought to solve, as a selectman. Little, inconsequential things that never amounted to a row of pins— Asey, is it eleven o'clock that's chiming? Oh, I've got to get to my shopping, right away! Asey, whatever are you going to do about things?"

Asey shrugged.

"If you could only find out who put that poison in the tarts," she said, "wouldn't that lead you to the murderer?"

"I think," Asey told her, "that's the way that Farley'll tackle this. It's the way he's already begun. Myself, I like the other angle better. If we can find out who killed Grove, then we can find out who strewed the arsenic around."

Tabitha seemed puzzled.

"Why is that a different angle?"

"B'cause," Asey said, "there's a lot more people who might have fooled around with the arsenic than people who might have killed Abner. You could spend a couple years tryin' to find out where an' when the arsenic got to those tarts, an' who got it there. But there's just one person that killed Grove, an' there's just a certain period of time when he done it, an' I think there's just one reason why he done it, too. Er—Tab, did you do any more sawin', around here? I mean, did you touch anythin' besides that cane?"

"No, Asey, I haven't touched another thing. That cane was the thing that caught my eye when I drove up. I just hopped out and grabbed it, and then I had to run back and turn off my car and put on the brake. I'd forgotten to stop. Asey, I simply must start off and get to my shopping—"

"Where is your car?" Asey strolled along beside her. "I never seen it."

"Over there, beyond the shed. Next month, I'm going to have a new one. That doesn't mean anything to you, you just have a new car every time Bill Porter puts out a new model, but I haven't had a new car in six years, and it means a lot to me—oh, don't try to open that door, Asey. That hasn't opened for two winters. I have to get in this side and wiggle over—"

After she had wiggled over behind the wheel, Asey politely shut the door.

Involuntarily, he looked at the back seat, and his eyebrows raised.

"What a lot," he said, "of nice, new shiny nails. From the looks of that boxful, you're goin' to go in for some renovatin', too."

"Oh, those nails!" Tabitha said. "Curtis left them at the house two weeks ago, after he fixed the back stairs, and I've been trying to get them back to him ever since. You know Curtis. I'd wait till doomsday if I waited for him to come and get them himself. Asey," her voice wavered, "was he killed here, here at his own house? It never entered my head that he might have been until I saw that cane lying there by the tub and the cistern."

"I hadn't thought it out as far as figurin' it happened right here," Asey said, "but I don't see no reason why not. Where's the rest of the cane you cut off?"

Tabitha pointed to a saw horse.

"There. Do what you think best about it. Asey, why haven't the police been here?"

"The workin's of the official mind," he said, "are somethin' I quit tryin' to grasp a long time back. I s'pose they're more interested in Banbury, right now, an' the arsenic problem. Like I said, Farley's workin' from that part to this. Tabitha, how come you happened over here?"

"I came to see about his dog," she said, "and then I remembered, he'd sent Jumper over to the vet's. He had a bad paw. Asey, you'll let me know the minute you find out anything, won't you?"

"I will," he promised.

He stood for a moment beside the shed and watched the old sedan bounce along the meadow road.

Those nice, shiny nails still bothered him. They were the

get frightened— Asey, can't you think of some-
can do? Dad said to keep mother's mind occupied.
e something we can hunt? I thought people always
ews, interminably. Can't we hunt? Haven't you
we can search for? Or comb? In stories, people
ys combing a house, or combing a room. Isn't
ething we can comb?"

rouble with combin', or huntin' for clews," Asey
that you got to have somethin' in mind to comb,
t's sort of like lookin' up the spellin' of a word in
ary. You got to have some idea of how the word's
efore you can find it. To be honest with you, I'm
ough trouble tryin' to sort out the things I've got
nd, without addin' any more just now. So—"

atch," Mrs. Banbury said.

watch?"

now, Asey, the one Dr. Cummings and I talked
er at your house," Jane said. "The presentation
omsie asked the same questions about the time he
l, and watches stopping, and all, that I did. And I
vhat Dr. Cummings said about Abner's not hav-
atch on. It's bothering her."

ainly is," Mrs. Banbury said. "Abner Grove had
e brought those tarts to the church supper last
he Welcome Wagon, because he took it out and
around at least a dozen times while he talked with
Abner's been seeing to the new traffic lights in
oon, and Phineas wanted to know about them,
e wiring was ready. That watch was one of the
ious possessions Abner had. I want to know what
f it."

Asey said, "if it'll brighten your lives to hunt for
atch, why, hunt away. I'd go easy on handlin' too
gs, because when the police finally get here, they
like it."

'll we start?" Jane said. "Truly, Asey, couldn't
a be a clew? Mightn't his not having it be sig-

ot?" Asey said.

y, he decided that he might as well humor the
women, since it looked as though he had been
eir keeper.

vell, we will," Jane said. "Momsie, shall we begin

same size as that nice, shiny nail that someone had tried to
ruin his back tire with.

Tabitha Sparrow might be convinced that she had not
an enemy in the world, but Asey was not so sure.

He walked over and looked at the two tubs of water
that stood in front of the cistern, and at the oyster shell
path that led from them to the house.

A hundred people might have walked, without leaving
any trace, over those closely packed shells. You couldn't
tell anything from them. Someone could have hit Abner
right there as well as anywhere else. And he could, con-
ceivably, have fallen in such a way that his head landed in
one of those tubs.

Thoughtfully, Asey turned and surveyed the house.

The front door was locked, but the door to the kitchen
ell opened as he turned the knob.

The electric light was still burning in the kitchen, and
another lamp burned in the dining room beyond. The tank
of the oil stove was empty, and the frying pan over one of
the burners had apparently been waiting to receive the
potatoes all sliced on the table. There was a pork chop on
a plate, too. A left-over, Asey decided. Abner had been
going to warm it up when he cooked the potatoes. Over on
the ledge by the soapstone sink was a can of peaches,
standing beside a well-worn can opener. Two tea bags sat
next to a brown glazed tea pot.

Asey rubbed the side of his nose reflectively, and then he
sat down in one of the straight-backed kitchen chairs and
pulled out his pipe.

Before he got it lighted, he heard footsteps on the
oyster shells outside.

Jane Banbury and her mother were walking up the path.
Lu Banbury smiled at him.

"Good morning, Asey! Well, they've taken Phineas off
to jail, and I've never been more relieved. The Lord knows
what this'll do to business, but I never was so glad to see
a man go to jail in all my life. At least, he'll be safe from
harm. No one can hurt him in jail."

"An' with him away," Asey held the door open, "they
let you leave Banbury Bog?"

"Not exactly," Jane said. "Momsie and I fiddled with the
drafts in the east room fireplace, and while the boys in blue
were solving that one, we left. Asey, I don't understand it.

I heard Farley say they already had a man at Grove's house—aren't there any police here? He—"

"I forgot to explain that," Mrs. Banbury said absently. "I'm afraid that's my fault. Farley asked me hours ago where Abner Grove lived, and I'm afraid I didn't make myself clear. I shouldn't be at all surprised if he hadn't sent his men to the house of that other Grove, on the other meadow in South Weesit."

"Momsie! That Grove that's no relation at all to Abner? You let him think—"

"I'm sure it's a perfectly natural mistake for a person to make,' Mrs. Banbury returned. "I once waited over there a whole afternoon for Phineas, one day when we first came. Farley had been terribly rude to your father, just before he asked me, and I thought it served him right to be made a fool of. D'you know, Asey, Farley never even noticed Jane had been away? He just thought she'd been taking a nap."

"Is Cummings over there?" Asey asked.

"Yes, he helped us get away," Jane said. "He had Farley's ear, and he was talking it off, being speechless about something. Asey, it looks as if Abner had been getting his supper, and then been interrupted, doesn't it?"

"Uh-huh. It looks that way."

"You mean," Mrs. Banbury said, "that he really wasn't? But everything's set out. Even tea bags."

"Uh-huh."

"And the can opener," Jane said.

"Uh-huh."

Mrs. Banbury frowned, and then she nodded briskly.

"Of course, how stupid of us, Jane! He'd never have made up his mind about two tea balls before he ate. Never. Or have decided on peaches. Look up on that shelf. See, there are other cans of fruit there. Abner never would have decided before a meal what he was going to have for dessert. He couldn't have. Isn't that what you mean, Asey?"

"I think you're right, Mrs. Banbury. If you didn't know Abner—say, if you was one of the cops—you'd just think that he'd just come home, an' was gettin' his supper, an' durin' the process, he got interrupted by an unexpected visitor."

"You mean Phineas," Mrs. Banbury said. "They'd say that Phineas came."

"Probably. But as a matter of fact, A[ ] supper up in the village last night. I fo[ ] when I was askin' questions around [ ] there, an' then he come home here."

"Now," Mrs. Banbury said, "I'm stu[ ] from there."

"Well," Asey said, "I'm inclined to [ ] after he ate, he come home here an' w[ ] come. I think he was expectin' a vi[ ] laid this stuff around so as if he was [ ] gettin' ready to eat a late supper, an' [ ] Say, while I think of it, I want to mal[ ] will you?"

He made two calls at the phone in [ ] whose door he casually shut behind hi[ ]

"So Tabitha's really got an alibi?[ ] returned. "I'm glad—"

"Have you been listenin' again?"

"We really couldn't help," Mrs. [ ] with the door closed. Did the girl [ ] phoned anyone to meet him here?"

"You're both eavesdroppers," Ase[ ] said he'd been calling Judge Chase."

"About that wood lot, I'm sure," [ ] once. "Abner was vacillating abo[ ] wanted it, but he wasn't sure of the [ ] told me all about it, several times, [ ] that the Judge was looking into it fo[ ] he called the Judge here to ask his [ ] known who put the arsenic in ou[ ] Judge to tell him what to do."

"Whatever he wanted him for,' [ ] made his mind up about one thing [ ] me. He had my number all written [ ] right over there by the phone. See [ ] get the number all written down."

"Then he did know who put th[ ] bury said. "Oh, if only he'd made [ ] thing about it earlier! If only he'd [ ]

"I wish he had," Asey said.

Jane, who had been roami[ ] kitchen, suddenly stopped and shi[ ]

"Every time I stop and think [ ]

with the attic or the cellar? In books, people always hunt from attic to cellar."

"Cellar," Mrs. Banbury said at once. "It's nearer. Is there a cellar, Asey? Where's the door?"

"It's that trap door,' Asey told her, "an I don't think I'd tackle it, if I was you. It's just a small, circular cellar, like all the old Cape houses got, an' there's probably rats—"

But Jane already had the trap door raised.

"We ought to have a flashlight," she said, "but I think my match flap will do for what investigating we'll do—oh, isn't this a funny little place! Momsie, come look."

The two of them disappeared down the ladder.

Asey sighed.

He had so much he wanted to get thought out, and the Banbury family was interrupting his thoughts. And they probably would continue to interrupt them, too, until he got Phineas Banbury out of this mess.

"Asey!"

"I'm busy," Asey said.

"Yes, but come tell us what this little door is. We can't open it, and we think it's a secret passage—"

"It's a door that'll lead to a cupboard," Asey said, "where they used to keep crocks of preserves an' jugs of molasses, an' such, in the old days. All those cellars have 'em—"

"This is different," Jane called up. "Come open the door! Asey, come open the door!"

Wearily, Asey went down the ladder.

"Where? That?" He tugged at the door and opened it. "There, see? Just what I said—"

The trap door above their heads banged suddenly into place.

CHAPTER VI

IN SOMETHING LESS THAN A
split second, Asey was up the ladder.

Just, Mrs. Banbury thought to herself, just like a cat. Just
as quick, and just as quiet. In the sudden and complete
darkness of the little cellar, she herself couldn't have told
even where the ladder was, without a lot of noisy fumbling
around.

She heard him grunt as he shoved against the door, and
then suddenly he was down beside her.

"Dear me," she said, speaking in a voice she hoped was
natural enough to deceive Jane, "dear me, has someone
gone and shut us up down here? Or shut us down, down
here? Anyway, are we shut up?"

"We can't be shut up!" Jane said. "We aren't, are we,
Asey?"

"It sort of seems," Asey said, "like we are. Now why'n't
I bring my pipe! Yes, Jane, it seems like someone must
have been waitin' outside, lurkin' around to grab just some
such chance as this. An' I must say, we certainly give it
to 'em!"

"Can't you shove that door open?" Jane put a foot on
the lowest rung of the ladder. "Can't I help you shove
it open? I've got quite a lot of the old Banbury muscle.
Come on, let's strong arm the trap door—"

"I'm 'fraid," Asey said, "that can't be done, Jane."

"Someone's just put something on the door, haven't they,
and weighed it down? Well, then, let's shove it off. Come
along."

"But it's locked," Asey said. "Someone's slid the bolt bar, Jane, an' there's no use tuggin' around. That floor's solid oak."

"I didn't see any bolts or bars!"

"It wasn't slid over," Asey said, "when you opened the trap door. Abner hadn't bothered to slide it over the last time he was down here. Well, well. I wanted a nice, quiet place to think, an' here it is."

"How perfectly silly," Mrs. Banbury remarked, "to have a bolt on that trap door! Why, what would anyone want with a lock there? There's nothing down here but this little circular hole. We can't get out, can we?"

"Not," Asey said, "without a lot of fancy tunnelin', an' I ain't equipped for it."

"Us," Jane said, "and Edmond Dantes. How many years did it take him?"

"Jane," Mrs. Banbury said severely, "don't think such things, and if you have to, please don't say them out loud. Asey, if we can't get out, no one could ever get in. Why should there be a bolt on that trap door?"

"There always is," Asey said, "in these ole houses. I got one on mine. I s'pose it was to make sure that the children wouldn't play with the trap door, an' fall down. It's like the bars on the attic windows in my house. The children used to sleep up in the attic, my father told me, when he was a kid, an' because the windows was only a few inches above the floor, they barred 'em. I once heard a real sensible man over home, tellin' people that those bars was because every family always had some crazy relation that had to be shut up somewhere, but that's nonsense. All these things that seem sort of queer now, they all served a purpose."

Jane touched the brick wall, and then drew her hand back from its clammy dampness.

"Why is the cellar round? Does that have a purpose too, Asey?"

"Sure. Bricks was mighty scarce in the old days, an' mighty expensive, an' you had to send to Boston, at least, for 'em. So you made the cellar of your house in a circle, instead of a square. Used fewer bricks, see? An' they made 'em with a single thickness, too."

"Really," Jane said, "you're not fooling us, are you?

Truly, did someone lock us in here? It just seems too crazy!"

"They did,' Asey saiu. "Listen. There, can't you hear footsteps? There's someone prowlin' around up there. Hear 'em?"

Jane and Mrs. Banbury listened.

They could hear the faint moan of the wind as it blew across the meadow and around the corner of the little half house, and the evenly spaced dripping of water from a pipe in the kitchen above.

"I can't hear a thing," Jane said. "Well, there's a train whistling—but I thought they'd stopped all the trains?"

"That's just a freight," Asey said, "or else maybe a sand train. Listen, now, can't you hear that?"

To him, the progress of the person upstairs had been perfectly clear and apparent. He could tell as much from those little squeaks and floor board creakings as though he had been standing in the kitchen, watching the person.

After slamming the trap door down, and sliding home the bolt, he had gone into the dining room for several minutes. Then back to the kitchen again. Then, after a period of apparent indecision, the soft-footed person had gone back to the dining room. Now, Asey decided, he was over in that corner by the telephone and the old desk.

"If there's anyone up there," Jane said, "he's walking on cotton batting, or else he hasn't any feet. Asey, this is all perfectly insane! Who could be up there? What could anyone want? Who is it? Why'd we get shut down here? Who is it?"

"Jane," Mrs. Banbury drew her breath in rather sharply, "can't you be content to think about cellars, and attic windows, and the scarcity of bricks in the old days, and things like that? Think of coming down this ladder here, in a hoopskirt, to get a cup of molasses. Was it Judge Chase or Evan who told us the story of the grandmother with the hoopskirts?"

"What grandmother with hoopskirts?" Jane asked. "I never heard a single word uttered about anyone's grandmother with hoopskirts. But I should like to know who is up—"

"Evan told us himself, and you were right there at the table," Mrs. Banbury said quickly. "He had a grandmother who loved hoopskirts, but she was afraid of thunder. She always wore the hoopskirts when she walked up to the village, but if it looked as though it might thunder before she got home, she stopped in at some neighbor's house, and took the hoops off in their shed."

"Silly wench," Jane said. "Why?"

"Because she had four brooks to cross before she got to her own house, and she was afraid that the combination of four brooks and steel hoops and thunder would all prove fatal. See?"

"No," Jane said, "I don't get it. Is it really funny?"

"What she means," Asey explained, "is that the woman was afraid of bein' struck by lightnin', an' it's an old country notion that water an' steel draws lightnin'. Got it now?"

"Yes," Jane said. "Is that all?"

Mrs. Banbury sighed.

"I must say," she said, "you've ruined a good story, between you. I thought it was such a nice story. I liked the picture of the woman scurring out of her hoops—"

"Momsie," Jane said, "one more word on the topic of hoopskirts, and Jane begins to yell. I shall yell—"

"I should think," Mrs. Banbury said, "that you might be able to evince a little interest in the grandmother of your elderly beau. And by the way, where is your elderly beau? I certainly thought that Evan would rally around."

Jane thought so too, and Evan's absence had bothered her enormously.

"He's not my elderly beau," she said rather crossly. "Momsie, I shan't be sidetracked! Who's upstairs? Who is it?"

Neither Asey nor Mrs. Banbury answered her at once.

"Oh," Jane said in a small voice. "Oh, you don't mean that it might be the—the murderer? You mean, he's up there this minute! Oh, how perfectly awful! What a perfectly harrowing thought!"

"It's your own fault," Mrs. Banbury said. "I told you to think about hoopskirts and things. I did my best. I tried to keep your mind off harrowing things. Asey, what on earth is that man doing?"

"Right now," Asey said, "I think he's goin' through the pigeon holes an' the drawers of Abner's desk there in the dinin' room. I can hear him teeterin' back an' forth on that loose floor board. I teetered on it myself when I was makin' those phone calls."

"What's he want? What's he after?"

"I s'pose," Asey said casually, "there's somethin' here that he thinks would be nicer out of the way."

"Was he watching us?" Jane demanded. "Was he listening to us?"

"Seem's if," Asey said. "I guess he come over the back of the hill, like I did, an' sneaked up from the rear. Then, when we all crawled down in this hole like good children, he popped us in. Good neat job, too. He thought quick, an' he acted quick."

'When," Jane inquired, "is Old Neat-and-Speedy going to let us out of here?"

Asey chuckled.

"Well, won't he? Asey," Jane said, "you don't think he's going to leave us here?"

"I don't think," Asey said, "that he's goin' to undo that bolt with a flourish, an' open up the trap door, an' invite us to have a good, searchin' look at him."

"Well, how are we going to get out?"

"Sooner or later," Asey said, "someone will drop by, an' then we'll raise our voices in song. Somethin' appropriate, but dignified. Like—let's see. Like, 'Let Us From the Darkness Now.' "

"I know that hymn!" Mrs. Banbury said. "Why, I haven't thought of that since I sang in the choir, and Phineas came to church twice every Sunday to hear me, in shoes that squeaked. Asey, let's practice!"

Over Jane's heated protests, Asey and Mrs. Banbury practiced the hymn.

"There!" Asey said. "If that harmonizin' don't bring the cops to their toes, nothin' will. Jane, wouldn't you like to learn the alto?"

"I certainly would not!" Jane said. "I think you're both perfectly awful. Why, mother, think! Father's in jail, and there's a murderer walking around over our heads, and you sit and sing hymns! Why, anyone might think you didn't care!"

"My dear child," Mrs. Banbury said, "your father is safe in jail, and we're safe here, and that's all that matters to me. Of course, I could stand here and cry my eyes out over what those headlines about arsenic may do to the Banbury tart business. But as long as we're all safe, I think it's just as sensible to sing, Jane. Asey, don't you think that some of Farley's men ought to be getting around here soon?

"Yes, an'—"

"And," Jane said, "what a lovely laugh this'll hand them! The great Asey Mayo—"

"Languishin'," Asey said, "in a small round hole. As a matter of fact, the cops aren't the only ones that're goin' to love this. I think our friend upstairs is probably givin' an occasional hearty snicker up his sleeve."

"You don't sound," Jane said, "as if it mattered to you. You sound as if you thought it was a good thing."

"I do," Asey told her blandly. "It suits me right down to the ground. Nothin' could happen that I'd like any better."

"Pooh!"

"No poohs about it," Asey said. "Don't ever forget, Jane, that there's a certain amount of value in bein' under-estimated by your opponents. We got a sayin' over my way that there's nothin' a skunk enjoys more than havin' some-one think it's sound asleep. You know," he added, "I told that to a lady reporter, once, an' she said wasn't that just too dear an' too quaint, an' too Cape Coddy. I thought it made a big impression on her, but it seems she missed the point, entirely."

"Why?" Jane demanded.

"Next night," Asey said, "she seen a cunnin' little cat sleepin' on the piazza of the place where she was stayin', an' she patted it. I'll pass over the ensuin' horrid details. Jane, where is your beau, Evan Chase? Oh, don't start snortin'. But ain't you got any stalwart boy friend that could come an' rescue us? I'm gettin' pretty tired of this dampy smell."

"We've got an awfully stalwart milkman," Mrs. Banbury said. "He virtually tears Banbury Bog apart, every morning. He could get us out of here with just one of those feet, and both hands tied behind him. But it's too late— Asey, why do you want to be underestimated?"

"This friend of ours upstairs," Asey said, "is bright. He plants Tabitha's blue enamel pin. He sends tart little messages on rocks. He swipes a nail from some Tabitha's got, an' sticks it in my tire. He lays out food in Abner's kitchen so as to give the cops a lot of wrong impressions an' untrue thoughts. An' now he's roamin' at leisure with us cooped up down here. He's an active soul, he is, just brim-min' with ideas an' vitality. It's my hope that he'll lose

some of his vitality, an' maybe have one too many ideas.
He—"

"Suppose," Jane interrupted, "that he's up there, now,
listening right over your head?"

"Oh, no," Asey said. "He's still around, but he went
outside about five minutes ago. He's scratchin' around in
the oyster shell path. Huh. Wonder what he's huntin' out
there?"

"Clews," Mrs. Banbury said. "I mean, things you might
think of as clews. Maybe he's hunting that watch—"

"I'm sorry," Asey said, "but maybe you hadn't better
bring up the subject of that watch again, Mrs. Banbury. I've
restrained myself real noble, but it ain't goin' to take a
lot for me to remind you that if there hadn't been some
thoughts about that watch, we wouldn't be here."

"I shall not," Mrs. Banbury said firmly, "utter another
word till we've got out. Jane, do you hear that? We've been
trying Asey beyond endurance. Now, don't say another
word."

"Oh, Momsie," Jane said, "Asey didn't mean it that
way—"

"Sh."

"But he—"

"I said sh," Mrs. Banbury retorted with great firmness,
"and I mean, shh!"

And, for the next hour and a half, there was silence in
the cellar.

For his part, Asey enjoyed it thoroughly. By the time
he heard the sound of a car coming over the oyster shells,
he had a great many things thought out in his mind.

"What was it we intended to sing—oho," he said. "We
don't need songs. I know the sound of that car. That'll be
my cousin Syl, in my ole Porter—"

"One more cousin," Jane said, "and I shall begin to
think the funniest things about your ancestors, Asey Mayo.
No human being can have as many cousins as you seem
to be able to produce."

"We been here a long time," Asey said. "You can collect
an awful lot of relations in three centuries—now, will you
cover your ears, please? I'm goin' to holler. I don't want
Syl to slip away."

He took a deep breath.

"Syl!" he bellowed.

"Asey!"

"Syl!"

"Asey?"

"How long," Jane inquired acidly, "can you two keep this up? Because my ear drums—"

"Syl, we're in the cellar! Unlock the trap door in the kitchen!"

"Huh? What say?"

Asey yelled for fully five minutes before Syl finally got the idea.

The sound of the bolt sliding off the trap door was one of the sweetest noises Jane had ever heard.

She helped her mother up the ladder, and blinked several times to get her eyes accustomed again to daylight. Then she looked at the little man with the walrus moustache who stood in the kitchen.

"My cousin Syl Mayo," Asey said. "Jennie's husband— tell me, Mrs. Banbury, are you really mad with me?"

She flashed him a smile.

"Not a bit. I knew you wanted to think in peace. I rather welcomed the lull, myself."

"Banbury?" Syl said. "You're the Banburys they're hunting for? Gee, Asey, Farley'll be mad when he finds out you've had 'em all the time! Gee whiz, won't he be good an' mad!"

Asey sat down in one of the kitchen chairs, and surveyed his cousin.

"Syl," he said, "are you tryin' to break somethin' to me easy? What are they huntin' these Banburys for? An', by the way, how come you are huntin' me? You *was* huntin' me, wasn't you? How in time did you ever happen over here? I thought you was out quohauggin'. Syl," he added parenthetically, for the benefit of the Banburys, "quohaugs. I thought—"

"Those clams," Mrs. Banbury said. "That's what you mean, isn't it?"

"No, mam," Syl told her seriously, "them ain't no clams. Them's quohaugs. Quohaugs an' clams is dif'rent. You see—"

"Syl," Asey said, "let's not get into that, now. Quohaugs, Mrs. Banbury, are the things that New Yorkers call clams. Let's leave it at that. Syl, you was out quohauggin', at last reports from Jennie, an' was due back tomorrow."

"Yup," Syl said, "but when I seen this fog, I says to myself, what's the use. So I come in just ahead of it—"

"Oh, fog!" Jane said. "That's the last straw. Fog!"

Mrs. Banbury sighed as she walked over to the window. "It *is* fog. Just billowing in. Just bounding in. And it was such a lovely, sunny day when we went into that cellar!"

"It's a Stayer," Jane said. "Oh!"

"That's what they was sayin' up in the village," Syl remarked. "They said it would be a Stayer. I thought so myself when I spotted the fog bank, an' that's why I told Sammy to start up the engines, an' we just brought the 'Emily' right in to the dock. Then I heard about Abner, an' all, so I left Sammy to take care of things an' went home to Jennie. An'—"

"An' Jennie told all," Asey said.

"Yup, she always knows everything. Every last thing," Syl said proudly. "So then I thought I might's well set out an' see if I couldn't help you, but nobody'd seen you or knew where you was. Farley said as far as he knew, you was in Timbuctoo. He seemed to think I'd know where you was, but I finally got Elnathan to tell him that I'd been out quohauggin' an' hadn't seen you for a couple days. N'en Elnathan asked me what I thought we ought to do about the Lodge next week—"

"Look, how did you know where I was? An'—"

"That's what I'm gettin' to," Syl said. "Abner had the Lodge books, see? Checkin' 'em. An' Elnathan said someone ought to get 'em, an' I said I would, so that's why I come here, see? I was awful surprised when I heard you yellin'. I hadn't seen the car around nowheres, an' I never thought you'd be here. 'Course, I s'pose I might have thought it out, but it seemed more likely to me that you'd been down on the shore, or over by the bog where he was killed."

"Huh," Asey said. "Well, it all goes to show you, I suppose, how things go. Syl starts to get the Lodge books, an' he finds us. Who knows, maybe if we hunt long enough for Abner's watch, we'll find our active friend— Syl, what's this about Farley huntin' the Banburys?"

Syl looked uncomfortable.

"Well, what?" Asey said. "What's up now?"

"Well," Syl said. "I— Asey, maybe I could speak to you alone for a minute, perhaps? Then—"

"If you're trying to spare us anything," Mrs. Banbury said in resigned tones, "just don't bother. After yesterday evening, and last night, and this morning, and that cellar, and now this fog, almost anything would be an anti-climax, as far as my feelings are concerned. Go on and speak right out. Just pretend we're not here, if it's something more in the nature of a catastrophe for the Banbury family. Let's get it over with."

"Well," Syl said, "I want to say right now, I don't be-lieve it. Seems to me that Banbury's done Weesit a lot of good, an' Jennie said you," he pointed to Jane, "was as nice an' pleasant a young woman as she'd ever met. An' you look nice, too, mam. I want you to know that's the way I feel."

"My God!" Jane said. "Momsie, it must be something simply hideous! Has—has Farley decided he wants to arrest us, too, along with dad?"

Syl tugged at his moustache.

"Syl," Asey said, "it isn't!"

"I guess," Syl said unhappily, "that just about sums it up. You see," he went on in a rush, "you run away. You—"

"We never did!" Jane said. "We walked. If the police hadn't been stewing around over a silly, smoking fireplace, they'd have seen us. But they were so scared of a little smoke, they just never thought about us at all. We walked out. In full daylight, and without any disguises or anything at all. Momsie, did we run away?"

"I can see," her mother said with perfect honesty, "where they might have got that impression, dear."

"An' then," Syl went on, "it seems you went to the bake shop yesterday afternoon, mam—"

"Of course I did," Mrs. Banbury said. "I told Farley so, myself. I went to see that Mawson didn't jam the racks—he's terribly careless. And he wasn't there, and I finally packed most of the tarts. Oh, I see. They think I had a hand in the arsenic, do they?"

"Yes'm. They claim your husband got the arsenic, an' you put it in the tarts then, when you was alone in the bake shop. I don't believe any of it, but—"

"What about me?" Jane said. "They haven't worked me in, have they?"

Syl began to look positively wretched, Asey thought.

"Have they?" Jane asked again.

"Well, you sort of went around at the supper," Syl said, "asking people to have more tarts. The little Rose boy, the Portygee kid that was so sick, he says he wouldn't have eaten any, if you hadn't persuaded him to have more."

"The mopper-upper," Jane said. "Well, well, well. Did you ever read any of the tourist literature father had printed, Asey? It's been handed out all summer, along with free tarts from the Welcome Wagon, and little tokens from Weesit's tradesmen. There's one sentence that's haunting me. 'Welcome to Weesit, where, as nowhere else—' "

" 'You will find,' " Mrs. Banbury said, " 'that true Cape Cod feeling of helpful, sincere, neighborly friendliness.' Is that the one you mean?"

"I meant the other. 'Welcome to Weesit, where, as nowhere else, you will find just one big happy family.' Oh, my God!" Jane said. "How I wish Dr. Cummings were here to be speechless for me!"

"Syl," Asey said, "does Farley actually intend to arrest Mrs. Banbury and Jane?"

"Yup. He—"

"Over my dead body he'll arrest momsie!" Jane said. "Dad can take it, but if he dares do anything to mother, I'll—"

"I certainly do not intend," Mrs. Banbury said, "to have my daughter arrested, Asey! Now, so far, I've tried to keep cool and not get mad, and be reasonable and philosophical, and all that. But if Farley tried to arrest Jane, I simply would not be responsible for my actions! It's one thing for Phineas. He'll make a marvelous story out of it, and have people roaring about the time he was sent to jail. But my daughter is not going to become a jail bird at twenty-three!"

"I—I haven't really told you all," Syl said. "There's more. That little Rose boy, he says he was in Tabitha's lane day before yesterday, an'—well, remember, mam, this is just what I heard. But he's told everyone, he saw you in Abner Grove's arms— "

"What!"

"So now," Syl said, "they're more sure than ever that the three of you killed Grove."

"That wretched child!" Mrs. Banbury said. "The one

I told you about, Asey. I was chasing him, and I ran full tilt into Grove—oh, don't I wish now that I'd caught that wretch! Don't I just wish I'd caught him!"

"Don't worry, momsie," Jane said. "I urged tarts on him, and he was the sickest of the lot, the doctor said. He—"

"Stop," Asey said. "Listen— Syl, d'you hear a motor-cycle? That's Farley coming—or one of his men. Mrs. Banbury, I want you—"

"Over my dead body," Jane said, "will that Potface arrest my mother—"

"If," Mrs. Banbury said simultaneously, "that man dares to arrest my daughter—"

Asey and Syl looked at each other.

"You better think quick," Syl said. "They're most here, Asey. I could go an' sort of stall 'em off—"

Asey pointed to the trap door.

"Down, Jane. Quick, Mrs. Banbury. Syl, lock that bolt behind us. You hang around, now, an' get us out the first chance you get. If they hang around too long, get doc, an' have him think somethin' up—hustle, Syl!"

With his pipe clamped between his teeth, and a kitchen chair in either hand, Asey scurried down the ladder into the circular cellar after the two Banburys.

Softly, the bolt shot home above them once again.

CHAPTER VII

SHORTLY AFTER SEVEN o'clock that evening, they heard the bolt slide back, and the trap door was cautiously raised.

Syl, with a finger at his lips, peered down at the three of them.

"Sh!" he said in a sibilant hiss, and then beckoned for them to come up the ladder.

With great haste, he led them through the wood house at the end of the kitchen ell, and out the side door. Then, with the air of a field marshal maneuvering great quantities of troops, he brought them to a halt out near the bushes where Asey had first seen Tabitha, earlier in the day.

Mrs. Banbury surveyed the thick, clammy fog which enveloped everything, and unconsciously shivered.

"I'm awful sorry, Asey," Syl said, "that you had to stay down there this long, but what could I do? There was that cop, sittin' right smack beside that trap door, an' there he sat, an' sat, an' sat—"

"We know," Asey said. "We—Jane, what is that thing you're grippin' to your bosom?"

"Peaches," Jane told him. "I grabbed that can of peaches when we went down, but I forgot to take along the opener. Is it still Thursday?"

"Sure," Syl said. "You ain't been there so terrible long. 'Course, I s'pose it seemed longish—"

"It seems," Mrs. Banbury said, "as though I'd spent the greater part of my life in that silly hole. I'm going to remember things about that cellar when I've forgotten my old red school house back in East Green Springs. Where are those police, just lurking around everywhere?"

"No, they just left that one cop behind," Syl said, "an' I finally talked him into goin' off an' gettin' some food—"

"Food!" Jane said. "Food. Remember, momsie? That stuff we used to put into our mouths and chew on. We used to have it three times every twenty-four hours, in the good old days. Momsie, I'm so starved, I could even eat a Banbury tart with relish."

Asey chuckled.

"I could eat one with mustard an' piccalilli," he said. "Syl, what was you shushin' us for at such a rate, if the cops has all gone?"

"I didn't want you to howl," Syl said, "like you did when I first come, an' I was sort of afraid that feller might pop back without really havin' got his food. I still think he may, because he didn't really want to leave, one bit. I just talked about food till he got hungry—"

"Yes, Syl," Asey said. "If you r'call, we was just underneath, with our tongues hangin' out an' our mouths waterin' —there was one time when you went into turkey dinners, an' I could have shot you. Syl, how'd they let you hang around? There's a lot of intervals that I missed hearin'."

"I told Farley I was a near relation of Abner's," Syl said, "an' I was waitin' for a call from another relation in Boston, to make funeral arrangements. That wasn't such a lie, in a way, Asey, because he ain't got any that I ever heard tell of."

"Any what?"

"Relations," Syl said. "But that means that the Lodge'll probably have to see to things, an' that means I'll be the one to see to 'em, in the end. Asey, those cops didn't find out anythin' attall here."

"I gathered that. Did they notice a cane, over by the sawhorse?"

"Yup. Farley said he must have been hard up for kindlin'. He just sort of gaped around, Farley did, an' then he told that feller to stay here in case Mrs. Banbury an' the girl should come here."

"How perfectly silly of him!" Mrs. Banbury said. "I'm sure that if Jane and I had any designs on Abner's house, we shouldn't attempt to proceed very far, with a policeman sitting in the kitchen rocker! Where are all the rest of those cops? What are they doing? Have they got anywhere?"

"Near as I can make out," Syl said, "Farley's got his fellers wanderin' around the bog, an' around the shore where the Welcome Wagon was—"

"What for?" Asey demanded.

"I dunno. Huntin' clews, I guess. Then he's huntin' the Banburys, too. Oh, an' he's sort of got his eye peeled for you, Asey. He told one of the other fellers to keep on watchin' for your car, an' then they got someone watchin' your house over home. Gee, I bet that'll make Jennie good an' mad, bein' guarded!"

"When," Asey inquired, "did I get into this mess? What do they seem to figure that I've done?"

"Well, to begin with, they ain't set eyes on you, an' they think that's queer. An' then they can't find the Banburys—"

"So they think I've whisked 'em away?"

Syl nodded.

"Seems to me," he said, "that the longer Farley doesn't find the Banburys, the more he thinks he's got to arrest 'em. It's kind of growin' on him, this idea that Mrs. Banbury an' Jane are guilty's all get-out. Say, Asey, is your car here? I want to borrow that tiny little screwdriver you got in your tool kit. Can I?"

He was so eager about it that Asey's curiosity was aroused.

"Sure you can have it, but what for?"

"It's that clock in there," Syl said. "The cuckoo clock Abner won to the Lodge raffle two weeks ago. It's stopped again, an'—"

"Clew," Mrs. Banbury said at once. "It's a clew. Clocks that stop are always clews. When did it stop?"

"Quarter-past nine," Syl said, "but I don't think that's any kind of a clew to anything, mam—"

"Of course it is," Mrs. Banbury said. "In books, there's always a clock stopping about the time of a murder. I've read it any number of times. It's always considered very significant."

"I think, mam," Syl said, "you're thinkin' about watches that stop when someone gets shot, or somethin' like that. But this is dif'rent. This's just a cuckoo clock that hangs on the wall in the dinin' room in there, an' Abner

won it in a raffle. Then, a couple days later, he brought it
over to my house an' asked me to see why it kept stoppin',
an' I tinkered with it, an' it went fine, an' I brought it back.
Then a couple days later, he brought it over again—"

"Is that the clock that Jennie was tellin' me about?"
Asey asked. "The one that's kept you awake nights?"

"Well," Syl said, "I bought it in the first place, an' there
wasn't no guarantee, but Abner thought it was my place
to make it go, an' keep goin', an' it went fine when I had
it, but when he brought it home, it kept stoppin'. Sometimes it went ten minutes, an' once it went for four days.
Anyway, I see it's stopped again, an' I thought I'd just
take that little screwdriver of yours, if you had it here,
Asey, an' give that dum clock just one more goin' over.
That dum clock's got my dander up. An' I ought to stay
here a while, because I promised that cop I would. He
was scared he'd get in trouble if Farley happened to telephone while he was up town after his food—"

Jane uttered a low moan.

"Hear that word again, momsie? Food!"

"Cheer up," Asey said. "You'll get food—"

"When?"

"Just as soon," Asey told her, "as I can get you an'
your mother straightened out. Settlin' you two in a safe
place is goin' to take some thinkin'. Now, I need—"

"My car?" Syl suggested. "They're watchin' for yours,
you know."

"Uh-huh, an' you said they're watchin' my house. So
that's out. An' this town is—" he started to say "poison,"
and then thought better of it. "This town is sort of a bad
place for you to linger in, right now. Syl, did you say that
the 'Emily' was at the dock? Well, then, you take Mrs.
Banbury an' Jane over to the 'Emily.' Then— "

"Food," Jane said. "Food. Remember? I don't seem to
be able to get that thought over. Momsie and I are starved."

"Syl'll get you food on board. Now, Mrs. Banbury, you
an' Jane get into Syl's car—where is it? Over here? Come
on. You an' Jane get in. With all this fog, you'll never be
seen, an' you can sort of stow yourselves away small on
the floor. When the cop comes back, Syl, you say you got
the call you was waitin' for, an' you got to leave right
away, an' make arrangements. Be awful bereaved. Then

take these two over to the 'Emily,' an' feed 'em, an' keep 'em there till I tell you to let 'em go. An' for Pete's sakes, don't drop in an' tell Jennie where you're goin', either!"

"But s'pose—" Syl began.

"If anythin' starts up that seems like it meant trouble," Asey said, "just slide the 'Emily' out into the bay. Keep them two out of Farley's way, see? Out of everyone's way."

Mentally, he added to himself, "Out of harm's way."

"All right," Syl said. "Say, could I take that clock along, Asey? I could tinker with it—"

"I sometimes wish," Asey said wearily, "that I hadn't ever given you that book on clocks, last Christmas, Syl. Yes, if the cop'll let you take that cussed clock, take it! Take anything that'll make you happy. Now, forget that clock for ten seconds, an' tell me. When you first drove out here, Syl, did you see anybody in the lane? Or around the road? Or in a car? Did you see anyone wanderin' around the general vicinity?"

"No." Syl shook his head. "Not a soul."

"Nobody? Sure?"

"Well, I saw Cousin Tabitha," Syl said. "She and that Milton woman was out at the turn, talkin'. Both in their cars."

"Anyone else?"

"Nobody," Syl said positively.

"Come on," Asey said. "Think hard. Who else did you see?"

"Why, there was Evan Chase. He was just below here, in his car."

Asey sighed. "I see," he said. "There just wasn't no one around at all."

"Well, those were folks I knew!" Syl said. "They don't count. I didn't see any strangers—"

"With long gray beards," Asey said, "an' black felt hats pulled over one eye in a sinister way. Yup. I see. I know what you mean. You didn't see no one except Tabitha, an' Mrs. Milton, an' Evan Chase. Er—did any of 'em consult with you?"

Syl thought for a moment.

"Tabitha waved at me," he said, "but Mrs. Milton didn't —well, after all, she don't know me only to say hello to. No reason for her to wave. An' Evan hailed me an' asked if I'd seen you, an' I said no, I was huntin' you myself. An' he said that you wasn't to Abner's—"

"Oh, he did, did he?" Jane said. "How would Evan know?"

"I s'pose," Syl answered, "he most likely drove out here as far as the turn, an' then when he didn't see Asey's car, he turned there an' went back. That's what I'd have done, if it hadn't been for those Lodge books."

"Didn't Evan say anything about us?" Jane demanded.

"Nope, he just said that about Asey."

"Well, dear," Mrs. Banbury said, "at least he's stirred himself to the point of asking about Asey. Maybe, sooner or later, he'll get around to asking about us. Hm. Asey, what are you going to do now?"

"I'm goin' to take my own car," Asey said, "an' go over to Banbury Bog an' chat with Farley, an' convince him that I got absolutely nothin' up my sleeve. Durin' the process, I'm goin' to find out what he's up to, or what he thinks he's up to, an' how he's goin' about it. An' I also want to find out what his experts think. Havin' done all that, I'll come over to the 'Emily' an' see you—now, you get in this car of Syl's, an' stay here. An' mind Syl."

"I wish," Jane said wistfully, "I had a can opener!"

Asey reached into his pocket and pulled out a large jack-knife, which he gave to her.

"One of the gadgets," he said, "is a can opener. If you get bored, you can play with the other dinguses. There's scissors an' a nice button hook, an' a compass—"

"And you had this all the time!" Jane said, stabbing at the can of peaches. "All the time we sat there starving in that cellar, you had a can opener, and you never told me!"

"All the time we sat there in that cellar," Asey returned, "you had a can of peaches, an' you never told me! Now, you be good, you two. An' for goodness' sakes, if you get any sudden, enlight'nin' impulses, don't follow 'em. Tell 'em to me when I come."

"We'll save them," Jane said, "for you— Asey, there's a car light on the road—see the glow over there?"

"It's that cop," Syl said. "Isn't it funny," he added meditatively, "the way a cop's car always has something the matter with a headlight, but then he'd bawl you out—"

"Syl," Asey said, "I'll wait over behind the shed till you

get started. Put on a good bereaved act for your cop, an'
—take care of these two, Syl!"

"Why, sure," Syl said. "Of course I'll take care of 'em.
Asey!"

There was one thing to be said about his bemoustachioed
cousin, Asey thought, as he made his way to the shed.
Syl's mind might not always work at any breakneck speed,
but he was a man who could be depended upon. If the
heavens fell and the earth belched forth fire, Syl would
somehow still doggedly manage to get the Banburys out on
the "Emily," and Syl would keep them there.

That was important, Asey thought, watching the cop's
car draw up. Keeping them there was very important. And
Syl would see to it that neither Jane nor her mother embarked on any of the impulsive enterprises of which they
were undoubtedly capable, if properly aroused. Syl would
keep them out of trouble, and, on the "Emily," they were
safe from trouble, too. Not just safe from the fear of arrest
by Farley, but safe from anyone else, like this active fellow with so many ideas. And it wouldn't be long, Asey felt,
before this fellow got around to thinking what a brainier
person would have thought of in the first place, that the
surest way to injure Phineas Banbury was through his wife
and daughter.

After considerable conversation with the trooper, Syl
finally got into his car and drove away.

Asey felt relieved to see it and the Banburys depart.
Relieved, and free. It seemed to him that great mobs of
people had been hovering around him all day long.

The kitchen door slammed behind the trooper, and
except for the occasional cry of a whippoorwill, the meadow
was quiet.

Slowly, Asey started up the slope to where he had left
his own car in the pine grove.

The thickness of the fog did not bother him in the least.
He had seen too much fog in his life. But, as he mounted
the slope, he shortened his steps and walked with care
around the clumps of bushes.

Finally he stopped altogether, and listened.

The whippoorwill in the meadow was silent, now, but
he could hear the engine of a car racing along the beach
road, and the sound of a bugle—that would be from the
girls' camp, he thought, over at Nauset Neck.

And that was all.

He couldn't hear a thing that might substantiate his feeling that there was someone besides himself on the side of that hill. No bushes rustled, no twigs creaked, no pine needles scrunched.

Cautiously, Asey started forward again.

By the time he reached the top of the incline, his forehead was hot and wet. His flannel shirt seemed to be glued between his shoulder blades.

But he had not heard a single suspicious thing. It was only his imagination, he told himself, that made his hands cold and his face hot, and his feet like hunks of lead.

His hand touched the cold, wet metal of his car bumper, and he felt along till he came to the door.

Unlocking it, he climbed inside behind the wheel. Automatically, his left hand locked the door behind him.

Asey drew a long breath and snapped on the fog lights, and then he started the car. No one, he decided, after listening carefully to the engine, no one had tampered with the motor. That was all right. Someone had tried the tires once; they probably wouldn't touch them again.

"Mayo," Asey said to himself, "you're an ole silly fool. An ole hungry fool. You get along with yourself!"

He leaned forward and twisted the button that turned on his windshield wiper, but the wiper blades did not work.

His hand was on the door knob before he remembered that the wiper blades had worked very efficiently the day before, during that shower in New Bedford. They always had worked very efficiently. Bill Porter was a crank about wiper blades.

"Oho!" Asey murmured. "Oho!"

He leaned back against the leather seat and laughed softly to himself.

Perhaps, after all, he had not been so very far from the truth.

There had been someone there on that hillside, whether he heard them or not. There was someone out there now, probably within reach of the car. Standing there in the fog, waiting.

"An'," Asey said, "I'm supposed to get out, an' crawl up on Bill Porter's fancy hood to fix them wiper blades, an' then you lean over an' sock me a good one. No, brother, not tonight. I ain't in the mood. But I'll give you credit for thinkin' up a good one. That was so easy an' simple, you come mighty near takin' me in."

He thought for a moment, and then he shook his head.

"Nope," he said regretfully, slipping the car into gear, "nope, some other time, brother, you an' me'll play games. Some time when I got my gun along, an' there ain't so much fog. I don't feel like playin' games now. I don't feel it'd be wise."

Within ten minutes, he was over at Banbury Bog.

Dr. Cummings hailed him loudly from the west porch.

"My God, where have *you* been? Are you after Farley?"

"I thought," Asey said, "that Farley was after me. That's what I heard. What's been goin' on, anythin' new?"

"Farley's men," the doctor said, "are all over the bog. In fact, a more bogged set of men I never saw. A bog is their natural habitat. They wallow in it. They like it there. They've found a stream they—"

"A what?"

"That crick," Cummings said. "The irrigation crick. They call it a stream, and they've come to the conclusion that's where Abner was drowned. They've found a nice stout stick they think he was hit with—of course, I've gone into the matter of blows with a blunt instrument, at some length, but that doesn't matter to them. They've embraced that stick. Asey, in all the days of my life, I've never seen such a disorganized affair! Why, Farley had some of 'em going over Albert Grove's house, on the Nauset meadow, half the day. He thought it was Abner's place. Good God!" Cummings thumped the porch railing with his fist. "Good God, Asey, think of it! They can't even find the *house* of the man who was killed. As I said to Farley, if he couldn't find that, how the hell could he expect to find the murderer?"

Asey chuckled.

"That was Mrs. Banbury's work," he said.

"Yes, Farley's got on to that. Asey, it's really a pity that a man who looks like such a brisk, clean-cut cop should be so—so obtuse! He—oh." Cummings broke off as Farley himself strode out on the porch. "Oh, hello. Here's Asey."

"I see him," Farley said. "How are you, Asey? Look

here, do you know where Mrs. Banbury and that girl are?"

"No, I don't," Asey said.

That, he thought, was true enough. He knew where Mrs. Banbury and the girl were going, but that was not what Farley had asked.

"I want them, Asey," Farley said. "I want them bad. If I could just get hold of them, then this thing would settle itself."

"So?" Asey said.

"This Banbury," Farley said, seating himself on the porch rail, "thinks he's a pretty big guy—"

"He is," Cummings said. "He's big, and he's all right, and you're making a grave mistake to—"

"Listen," Farley said irritably, "will you let *me* talk for a change? Banbury thinks he's too big to touch, but he isn't. He feels pretty safe about this business of being arrested. He thinks, when he feels like lifting his finger, then Judge Chase'll pull wires to get him out. He thinks this is all funny. But he'll change his tune, if I can just get hold of his wife and his daughter! He'll change his tune, then. He's pretty fond of his wife and daughter. He'll feel different when I take them to jail!"

Asey pulled out his pipe.

"Oh, I see," he said. "You're goin' to make Banbury talk by arrestin' them?"

"That's psychology," Farley said.

"It's damnfoolery nonsense!" Cummings said. "That's what it is! You haven't one speck of proof that Banbury's guilty of anything! All you've got is a little circumstantial evidence, like arsenic in the cellar. You haven't one ounce, one iota of proof! Absolutely nothing has happened that could make you think that Phineas Banbury is guilty of anything! Not one damn thing has happened—"

"That's just it!" Farley snapped. "Nothing's happened. Why? Because, Banbury's not had a chance to do anything, that's why! He's in jail. And so nothing's happened!"

Asey, as he filled his pipe, thought of the blue enamel pin, and the rocks, and the notes, and the nail in his rear tire, and Abner's trap door slamming down over their heads, and the windshield wiper.

"And now," Farley said, "I'm going to make Banbury break down and change his tune. I didn't think it'd be necessary to bring those women to jail and let him see 'em. I thought if I just let him know I was going to arrest 'em, that'd be enough. I thought he'd break down then. But he didn't—"

Asey stopped filling his pipe, and stared at Farley.

"Did you—you didn't tell Banbury you was going to hold them? You did! What did he say?"

"Well," Farley said, "he didn't say anything. He didn't seem to care. He just asked for another cup of coffee. He thought I was bluffing."

"I see," Asey said, stuffing his pipe back into his coat pocket. "I see."

"So," Farley went on, "that's why I've got to get hold of those two women, and let Banbury see I mean what I said. Honestly, Asey, haven't you got any idea where they are? You ought to know something."

"Me," Asey stood up, "I've spent the day in a cellar, Farley, not havin' very many ideas about anythin'. Was that all you wanted to see me about, just them two?"

"Yes, that and—oh, hell, is that the phone for me again, Bill? Wait'll I get back, will you, Asey?"

Cummings looked at Asey, as Farley followed a trooper back into the house.

"There," he said. "See what I mean? Bogged, and he likes it. He thinks it's fine. He—what's the matter with you, man?"

"Did you hear that, doc?" Asey said. "He told Banbury he was goin' to arrest his wife an' daughter, an' Banbury just said he wanted some more coffee. Oho! Doc, I got to do some plan changin', mighty quick! I didn't see Banbury over such a long space of time, but he ain't the sort to ask for another cup of coffee when someone tells him a thing like that! No, siree! I got to get them two an' take 'em up to see Banbury, quick, an' stop him b'fore he gets started! Good lord, doesn't Farley know he's just as good as touched off a volcano? I got to hurry an' get them up an' have 'em persuade him to—"

"Why, you can't!" Cummings said. "Are you crazy? You can't take those two women to him! And what can Banbury do, anyway? What do you mean?"

"I got to take 'em," Asey said. "I'll wangle it somehows. I got to! Why, doc, you can't tell what Banbury'll do, if he thinks that anything like that is likely to happen to his family! I know. I already seen what the other side of that family thinks of him, an' he—"

Farley burst out on the porch.

Asey took one look at him, and began to walk toward his car.

"Do you know what's happened?" Farley shouted. "Do you know what's happened?"

"How long ago," Asey paused on the path, "did it happen? When did he go?"

"They don't know! They just found out—say!" Farley glared at Asey. "How did *you* know? How'd you know he'd broke jail?"

CHAPTER VIII

"How'd you know?" Far-
ley yelled.

Asey opened the car door, and smiled at him.

"How'd you know?"

"Psychology," Asey said. "Element'ry psychology. So
long."

Dr. Cummings bustled down the path to the car.

"Asey, wait! Wait, man! Wait, will you? Asey, hold
on!"

"Can't wait. I got things to look after—"

Cummings jumped on the running board and stuck his
head into the car.

"Wait, Asey, I've got something to give you. Lean over
here. Jennie gave it to me when I dropped in over at your
place this afternoon. She said that if the police had already
begun slinking around, watching your house, there was no
telling who else might slink and watch, and you'd better
have it. Here. Don't let Farley see. It's your old gun."

"Thanks."

Asey slid the old-fashioned single action Colt into his
belt.

"Don't you want me to go along with—"

"Nope, you string along with Farley, doc," Asey said. "I
want to see how he's goin' to figure this one out. Oho.
Wait—"

"What's the matter?"

"There's a look on Farley's face," Asey said, "that I
don't care for. He knows I'm up to no good, an' I got

this feelin' he might even have someone follow me. See if he's got any ideas like that, an' if he has, see if you can concentrate his thoughts on my house, will you? Bait him."

"Gladly," Cummings said.

Farley's eyes narrowed as he watched the yellow glow of Asey's fog lights cut a swath down the driveway.

"Some one of these fine days," he said as Cummings returned to the porch, "that guy's going to have a crack-up, the way he drives. Well, I know what he thinks, and he's going to get stung. He thinks he knows it all, but this is the time he gets fooled. He don't know everything this time."

"No?" Cummings said.

"No! He thinks he can race off and get Banbury, all by himself," Farley said. "He hasn't got any credit out of this mess yet, and he thinks he can get some credit if he finds Banbury first. Well, that's where he's all wet. They already got a posse out looking for Banbury—"

"Scouring," Cummings said.

"What?"

"A posse," Cummings informed him, "scours. They don't look, Farley. They scour. My God, you don't even know the proper language!"

"Yeah?" Farley said. "Well, just the same they got a posse out, and they're stopping all cars coming down the Cape—"

"And so," Cummings said with lavish irony, "and so, Asey will never get the credit for picking Banbury up. My God, Farley, but you're a stupid man! Whatever makes you think that Asey'd ever try to go wandering off, up the Cape, to find Banbury? Why should Asey go the hell and gone—" He stopped short and bit his lip. "Well, on the other hand, maybe you're right, Farley. Yes, yes, maybe you're right, Farley. For all I'd know, Asey does plan to go up the Cape and hunt Banbury. Yes, yes, indeed!"

Farley smiled broadly.

"I guess, doc," he said, "that's the place where you went and gave yourself away, isn't it? Asey thinks that Banbury'll make for him, doesn't he? I get it! Well, we'll settle that!"

"What are you going to do?" Cummings tried to make his voice properly anxious.

"Well, I was going to phone someone to watch at the

Orleans four corners, and trail him if he went up the Cape from there. But now I'll do better than that. I'll just post a few men around Asey's house. And then, if Banbury manages to get through that posse, and somehow hooks a ride down without being picked up on the way, well—there he'll be."

Cummings, with great care, selected a cigar from his case.

"Have one, Farley? No. Okay. Well, Farley, if you think it's a good idea to surround Asey's house, I suppose it's a good idea to surround Asey's house. But I don't know but what your first thought was better. Well, well, I've got to be getting on, I guess—"

"No, you don't!" Farley said.

"No, I don't what?" Cummings said. "If you mean I don't go, you're crazy. I've got my calls to make! Get out of my way!"

"Calls!" Farley said. "You're going to get the hell out of here and go tell Asey what I'm going to do. I know you. Well, you're going to stay right here, see?"

"My calls have got to be made," Cummings said. "I've got patients who—"

"If anything urgent comes up," Farley said, "I'll let you go. And I'll send a man with you to see that you don't drop any notes around or make any phone calls, warning Asey. And in the meantime, you stay right here."

Cummings looked at him, and then sat down in the most comfortable porch chair.

"All right," he said. "I won't argue with you. I shan't say a word. I'm too speechless to say a word. But mark my words, Farley, you'll hear plenty if old Mrs. Higgins' shoulder gets worse. You'll hear plenty if Salvatore Silva's wife has another set of twins. You'll hear plenty if anything serious happens to my patients. You'll take the blame. I won't! Can I make a phone call?"

"No. If you've got any calls, I'll make 'em for you."

"All right," Cummings said, "phone my wife and tell her she'll have to get another fourth for bridge. I'm detained."

Tilting his cigar at an angle in the corner of his mouth, Dr. Cummings closed his eyes and leaned back in Phineas Banbury's favorite chair.

The incoherent sounds of wrath issuing from Farley's

throat gave him a vast amount of pleasure. He still had no idea of what Asey was up to, but Farley had been baited. And baited, the doctor thought, rather well. And if Asey had proceeded at his usual speed, he ought now to be well along up the Cape. Even with the fog, he should have passed beyond Orleans.

As a matter of fact, Asey had stopped on the outskirts of Weesit, at the crest of the long hill.

He barely had finished lighting his pipe before a trailer truck started up the long grade.

At the top of the hill, Asey stopped it.

"Pull over—"

"Listen, buddy," the driver said, "I been searched. I been searched five times in the last thirty minutes. For God's sakes, can't you guys pick a—oh, hell, you're no cop! What you mean—"

"Hold it," Asey said. "Are they stopping all trucks—"

"They're stoppin' every damn thing. Trucks, cars, baby carriages—say," he added belligerently, "what's it to you? What do you want to know for?"

"I just heard that they was stoppin' trucks," Asey improvised rapidly, "an' I wanted to find out what for, an' if they was stoppin' all trucks. 'Cause I got my truck all loaded with fish, see? An' I wondered if I could get by, on account they warned me last week about the brakes, an' I ain't had time to get 'em fixed. I thought I'd be able to run her up tonight okay—"

"You'll be okay goin' up, buddy. They're just stoppin' 'em comin' down the Cape. They won't bother you goin' up. Seems some guy broke jail, up the line, an' they're tryin' to get him."

"Then it ain't another of these sneak inspections?" Asey said.

"No, they're just after this guy, an' they're sure he'll be comin' down this way, that's why they're just stoppin' the down Cape traffic. You'll be okay if you're goin' up, buddy. They won't never stop you goin' up."

"Thanks, feller," Asey said.

He stood by the roadside as the truck started rolling down the hill, and then he crossed over and walked slowly to where he had left his car.

Phineas Banbury was no fool. Everyone expected him to come down the Cape. Banbury would know that hordes of police were waiting for him to come down the Cape and walk right back into their clutches. Apparently it never entered anyone's head that Banbury might go to any other place in the world except Weesit, down the Cape.

"So," Asey murmured to himself, "he won't do any such thing. Mr. Phineas Banbury will go up the Cape, instead."

It was the only thing to do, under the circumstances. In Banbury's place, Asey would have gone up to Boston without any hesitation at all. The method and the speed of returning to Weesit would depend very largely on the strength of Banbury's desire to get back there. Ordinarily, he could take a boat or a plane. In fact, Asey thought, he wouldn't put it beyond Phineas Banbury to sail down from the sky above Banbury Bog in a parachute.

There was only one joker, and that was the fog. That changed everything. It would make a plane impossible, and it would slow down a boat to a point where Banbury might as well stay in Boston and wait for the fog to clear, and take a plane anyway.

That, Asey decided, was probably what Banbury would do. In any event, as long as there was this fog, and as long as all the cars coming down the Cape were being stopped, Asey would not have to worry about what might happen to Banbury. If cars had been stopped in both directions, Asey would have continued on and tried to take a hand. But Banbury had sense enough not to walk into a trap. And, as long as the fog held on, Banbury was pretty much stopped.

Asey turned his car around and started back over the hills toward Weesit.

Parking outside Tabitha's orchard, Asey went around to the back door and knocked.

"If it's Freddy with the clams," a voice announced, "leave 'em."

"It's me, Asey Mayo—is Tabitha in?"

Mary, Tabitha's first assistant, came to the door.

"Oh, hello. You want Tabitha? She went over to Marian Milton's, about half an hour ago. I thought you was Freddy with the clams. I don't see where that man is! Old Mr. Abbott's going tomorrow, and I promised him a sea clam pie for lunch, and I shan't feel right till I got those clams in the ice box. If you see Freddy, Asey, I wish you'd tell him to hurry right along with 'em!"

"Sure." Asey didn't know who Freddy might be, but he was perfectly willing to be obliging. "Say, I see you got one of Jennie Mayo's pies there. Ain't that apple pie one of Jennie's?"

"It is not, it's one of my own there on the table!" Mary returned.

"You don't say!" Asey said. "I didn't know anybody could make as fine a lookin' pie as that, outside of Jennie. Looks like it tasted just as good as hers, too."

"Asey, are you tryin' to ask me for a piece of pie?"

"I'm tryin'," Asey told her honestly, "to work a whole meal out of you, if I can. I ain't had a thing since breakfast—"

"For land's sakes, come in!" Mary said. "Whyn't you say you was hungry, instead of goin' through all that rigamarole about my pie! Come in, come in—"

Asey watched her as she bustled around the kitchen.

"Mary," he said at last, "what do you think of all this mess about poisoned tarts, an' Banbury, an' Abner Grove?"

Mary shrugged.

"Why ask me?"

"Well," Asey said, "I s'pose I can wait for Freddy the clam man, an' ask him."

"What d'you think he'd know about it, that half-witted thing?"

"Probably," Asey said, "he won't know much, Mary, but I got this hankerin' to talk things over with someone outside the family circle, as you might say."

"You sound like Judge Chase," Mary said. "He's always as-you-might-saying about something."

"Well, you know what I mean. If I thought that Phineas Banbury was to blame for everything, I couldn't very well say so to Mrs. Banbury an' Jane. Or Tabitha, or the Judge, or Mrs. Milton. They'd just get huffy. I been just kind of wonderin' what folks really thought."

Mary pursed her lips as she stirred cream sauce in a pan on the stove.

"Well, I don't think Banbury's guilty of anything, Asey. But there's an awful lot of folks that does. They say he started out all right, but now he's just gone crazy. I don't know why they think that. It's sort of like you think a president is fine, and then he starts in doin' all sorts of outlandish things. But I don't think Banbury's guilty of anything. I think someone's just out to do him harm. I think someone else put the poison in those tarts. I don't think he did. Land's sakes, as I told Phrone, that man ate here three weeks, and then off an' on till they got their house done, and I guess if he wanted to poison anyone, he could have begun here. He was in an' out of the kitchen enough. He's a good cook, too. Showed me a fine gravy."

"I been wonderin'," Asey said tentatively, "about that Marian Milton."

Mary put both hands on her hips and stared at him.

"Why, Asey Mayo, I'd just as soon begin to wonder about Tabitha! Marian Milton's an awful good person, and I don't think folks begin to appreciate what she's done for the town. She's given people jobs in her hooked rug place, and she's always taken an interest in town things—"

"Seems to me," Asey said, "I heard somewheres that she was all the time harryin' Abner Grove. That so?"

"Why not? *Some*body had to harry him and the other selectmen. Why, until Banbury came, the only way anything got done around here was to plague the selectmen till they did it! She's always taken a real interest in the town, Marian has. Of course, she couldn't make the sort of splurge that Banbury did, with all his money, but she's done a lot. She's a real nice person when you get to know her. As I said to Phrone this morning, Marian Milton did just as much within her means as Banbury."

Asey nodded judicially.

"I s'pose you know her better than I do," he said, "but just the samey, I wish I knew about last night."

"What about—oh, my sauce, I forgot it! What about last night?"

"Where she was," Asey said. "Yes, sir, I wish I knew where she was last night around nine o'clock, or a little later."

"Well, I can tell you," Mary said. "She was right up to the post office, getting the mail. That's where. Both of us hurried in just before they closed the office up, and we just made it. Lucky for us, because we both had to get a package at the window. So there! That's where she was!"

"They close the office at nine, do they?"

"Yes," Mary said. "And then we walked down the street

together, and we stopped and chatted with a few people—
I tell you, you needn't think anything suspicious about
her."

"Well," Asey said, "that's helpful of you, because now
I only got to wonder about Judge Chase. An' I ain't goin'
to wonder much about him. I think he's all right."

He was going to sound out public opinion, Asey thought
grimly, if it took him all night. He had intended to take
his soundings early that morning, but Abner's confounded
cellar had intervened.

Now that he had Mary available, he was going to find
out what Mary thought. For what he wanted to know, her
thoughts would do as well as anyone's.

"Yes, I guess the Judge is all right," he said again.

He could tell from the set of Mary's back, as she bent
over the stove, that Mary did not think so one bit.

"That's what Tabitha says," Mary said with a sniff.
"Tabitha thinks he's a fine man."

"Don't you?"

"I think," Mary laid a plate before him, "he's an old
scoundrel. That's what I think. All Chases are scoundrels.
They feel so high and mighty, and they're no better than
common thieves!"

"Mary," Asey said, "it seems to me you're kind of bitter
about Chases. Most people think they're a real upstandin'
family."

"Most people," Mary retorted, "don't live next door to
'em, the way we have! Asey, haven't you ever heard about
our east boundary? You never did?"

Mary promptly launched into the history of the east
boundary. It began, as far as Asey could make out, shortly
before the War of 1812, and apparently the controversy
had lasted, with unabated intensity, up to the present day.
And it had involved practically every member of Mary's
family, and almost every Chase in Weesit.

"So," Mary said, "there's that twelve-foot-strip. A hundred and fifty feet long, and twelve wide. And Judge Chase
won't give in, any more than his father would, or his
grandfather either. Scoundrels, the whole lot!"

Asey murmured something soothing about the land court.

"Land court! We live there— Freddy, is that you?"

After a brief conversation through the door, Freddy, the
clam man, came into the kitchen.

He was a tall, gangling individual, and his rubber boots had the longest feet that Asey ever recalled having seen. In his right hand, stiffly extended in front of him, was a quart measure.

"No container again!" Mary said. "Oh, dear me, why can't you manage to have containers?"

"Cost money," Freddy said succinctly.

"But that old tin thing! Do you know Asey? Asey, this is Freddy Higgins."

"Evenin'," Asey said.

Freddy inclined his head in Asey's general direction, but that was the only effort he made toward acknowledging the introduction.

"Look out, look out, you're spilling those things!" Mary said. "Here, give 'em to me and let me put 'em in a pitcher— Asey, I thought you intended to ask Freddy what he thought."

There was a challenge in Mary's voice. Clearly, Mary did not feel that Freddy thought.

"So I did," Asey said imperturbably. "Tell me, what's your idea about all this mess in town, Freddy? The poisoned tarts, an' Grove, an' Banbury. All that business."

Freddy shrugged.

"Ask him," Mary suggested, "what he thinks about Judge Chase."

"What do you think about Judge Chase?" Asey inquired obediently.

A gleam of something akin to intelligent interest appeared in Freddy's eyes.

"I think Judge Chase's just about the best man we got in this town," Freddy said.

"Go to bat for him, do you?" Asey said.

"Talk all you want to about this Banbury," Freddy said. "It's Judge Chase kept this town goin'. He give people jobs. Took an interest in things. Kept after the s'lectmen till they got things done. Deserves just's much credit as Banbury, the Judge does. Folks don't appreciate him like they ought to."

"Well, well!" Asey said in some surprise. "You go all the way, don't you?"

"You want to know why?" Mary demanded. "Freddy thinks that because the Judge got him off paying some fines for taking too many clams. That's why."

Asey grinned.

"How d'you feel about Mrs. Milton, Freddy?" he asked.

Freddy made a face, and clamped the thumb and fore-finger of his right hand over his nostrils.

Mary almost threw the empty tin measure at him.

"Get out!" she said. "You mean thing! Get along out of my kitchen!"

"Fifty cents," Freddy reminded her.

Mary took a fifty-cent piece from a cup on the window sill.

"Here. And the next time, bring your clams in a clean container!"

"Night," Freddy said.

Asey chuckled as the door closed behind him.

"Quite a lad, Freddy is," he said. "I can't imagine how I ever missed seein' Freddy before. Or his feet."

"You've probably seen him," Mary said. "He spends most of his time holding up the front of the post office. With his shoulder blades. He hates Marian Milton because she fired him, he was so slow and stupid running errands. And he thinks the Judge is the finest man—Asey, doesn't it beat all, what people think, and why they think it?"

Asey smiled at her.

"Public opinion," he said, "is always amazin'. Jennie can't stand that Pettigrew man over in Wellfleet, an' she claims it's because of his gold tooth. An' at the same time, her dearest friend, Nettie Sears, has a mouth full of gold teeth. Mary, thank you kindly for my supper. Your pie's as good as Jennie's, an' I can't give more praise than that."

"You going to find Tabitha?" Mary asked. "Well, you won't tell her what I said about the Judge, will you? She won't let me say a word against him. That's the only thing I have against Tabitha. She likes the Chases."

Asey picked up his yachting cap.

"Seems to me," he said, "Tabitha's as well liked as anyone in town."

"Well, I guess she *is!*" Mary said. "Just let anyone say a word against her, at least when I'm around. She hasn't an enemy in the world."

Asey stuck his yachting cap on the back of his head.

"Mary," he said, "if I was to ask you who was most important in this town before Banbury come, who'd you name?"

"Marian Milton," Mary said promptly. "And Tabitha. And—well, I s'pose Judge Chase. All of 'em tried to keep things going. But somehow, Banbury just got things done. And they went off just as slick, and easy!"

Asey nodded. He had no doubt that Phineas Banbury's exit from jail had also gone off slick and easy, too.

"I know what you mean," he said. "Where's Mrs. Milton's house?"

Mary's directions were lengthy, and full of good solid details, like white houses with green shutters, and picket fences, and elm trees, and hydrangea bushes, and flagstone walks. But, Asey thought, as he braked at the dead end of a lane, Mary's directions would work better on a night with less fog. When enveloped in a Weesit Stayer, one hydrangea bush looked very like another.

Turning the car around, Asey made his way back to Main Street.

The clerk in the drug store gave him a new and less involved set of directions.

Asey followed them to the letter, but this time he landed in what appeared to be the town dump.

The clerk laughed when he returned to the drug store.

"Haven't you got there yet?"

"Listen," Asey said, "let's get back to landmarks. The way I figure this out, Mrs. Milton ought to live somewheres near the old Knowles place."

"It *is* the old Knowles place," the clerk returned, "but Banbury had a new lane laid out—"

"Don't tell me," Asey said. "It's these new lanes that got me off. I can find the old Knowles place in my own way."

His own way would have worked out beautifully, except that with the passage of years, the old Knowles place had been turned around.

He had parked, Asey discovered as he stepped out of the car, between two flower beds at what was now the rear of the house.

Stepping gingerly between the marigolds, Asey started around to the front of the house.

He spotted the outlines of the picket fence Mary had made such a point of telling him about, and he bumped into one of the elm trees.

Then the hydrangea bushes loomed at him.

Then, he saw the man.

CHAPTER IX

SIMULTANEOUSLY, THE
man beside the hydrangea bushes seemed to become aware
of Asey.

"What—"

Both of them spoke the word at the same time.

Then, suddenly, the man beside the bushes rushed
full tilt at Asey.

Almost before he knew what had happened, Asey found
himself spilled on the ground by a violent straight-arm
tackle. Spilled with such a jolt that every bone in his body
ached, and his teeth felt loosened.

And the man was racing away through the fog.

Asey got to his feet, listened, and then started after him.

He had been right, he thought as he ran along, following
the sound of the racing footsteps ahead. He had been right
about the bright ideas and brimming vitality of this fellow.
Here was a lad who was quick on the uptake. No hesitat-
ing for him. No stopping in the fog for a quiet chat. No
jockeying around or slinking stealthily away. Just wham
and whoosh. That was him.

Remembering the elm tree, Asey swerved just in time
to miss bumping it again. He was beginning to wonder
about the location of that picket fence, when a bump
and a thud and a grunt from somewhere in front of him
told him that his friend, the vigorous lad, had already
stumbled on it.

Asey increased his speed.

Six feet ahead of him, the man arose from the ground

with all the resiliency of a rubber ball, and, hurdling the fence, started off once again.

"Playful!" Asey murmured, and followed him over the fence.

He never saw a man more eager to play and race around. Now that he had his gun, Asey felt more willing to join him, but when you came right down to it, the gun was of very little use to him now. He could blaze away at a sound in the fog, of course. He could always potshot around, smash a few windows, pink a few innocent by-standers, arouse the neighborhood and start them phoning wildly for Farley and the cops.

But, Asey thought, it was highly unlikely that he would hit this man.

"Huh," Asey said, and stopped.

The man had far outdistanced him. He must know this region like the inside pocket of his coat, to rush around in a bee-line in spite of the fog. If it weren't for the feeble glow of a single street light ahead, Asey himself would not have been able even to hazard a guess as to the direction in which he was facing.

But this fellow had gone streaking like a bullet over toward Main Street, and that new lane of Banbury's.

A car started up, and the engine was raced provocatively.

"Oh, go along with you!" Asey said. "You got too many ideas, you have! You ain't goin' to egg me on into any nasty ole ambush! No, sir. Go along with you!"

Turning, Asey strode back to the old Knowles house.

There was a light burning in the living room, but no one answered the tattoo he beat on the wrought-iron front door knocker.

Asey banged again.

"Mrs. Milton," he called out, "it's Asey Mayo!"

There was a short silence, and then a voice piped up from inside.

"What?"

"Asey Mayo, Mrs. Milton!"

He grinned as he heard a chain slide off its guard, and a key turn in the lock.

Somehow, he had not thought of Mrs. Milton as being the kind of woman who quaked at a knock on the door. After all, it wasn't late.

"Asey!"

Tabitha and Mrs. Milton both stood in the hallway by the door.

"Asey, come in!" Tabitha said. "Come in, quick! Don't stand there in the light—come in!"

She pulled him in, and Mrs. Milton hastily replaced the chain, and turned the key.

Asey stared curiously at the pair.

"What's the matter?" he demanded. "What're you two shaking so for?"

"We're f-frightened," she said. "Asey, we're frightened to death! Somebody meant what they said in those notes they left under the rocks on our doorsteps!"

"What's happened?"

"There's been someone outside trying to get in," Tabitha said, "and—"

"He tried the back door," Mrs. Milton interrupted. "And the cellar window. And he started to climb the trellis! Asey, we've been terrified!"

"You look," Asey said, "as if you'd been petrified. Tabitha, why'n time didn't you march straight to the phone an' call someone?"

"We tried to!" Tabitha said. "What do you think, Asey, do you think we're utter fools? We tried to phone, but we can't get central. We think the line's been cut."

After a few minutes of fruitless fiddling with the phone, Asey agreed.

"But is that all that's happened? Is—"

"Isn't that enough?" Mrs. Milton inquired acidly. "The phone cut, and some prowler trying to get in, and all this fog? We didn't dare go out—"

"I've been ready to go home for an hour and a half," Tabitha said, "but I didn't dare walk out to my car. Oh, it's all right for you to stand there and grin, Asey Mayo! You think we're just two silly foolish females. But you've got a gun. And we didn't have anything more deadly to brandish than the fire poker and that flintlock Marian took down from over the mantel!"

Asey looked at the musket and the long fire poker, sitting on the table, and grinned more broadly than ever.

"If I'd been your prowler," he said, "an' seen you two comin' toward me brandishin' them things, I'd have fled. Trouble is, Tabitha, you just didn't make the most of your op'tunities. You always could have tossed a little boilin' water out of an upstairs window—boilin' oil's the thing, of course, but water would have done—"

"We did," Mrs. Milton said. "That's how we stopped him coming up the trellis. Pails of boiling water, and pepper."

Asey sat down on the couch and rocked with laughter.

"Oh, my," he said, "I wish I'd got here earlier! My, I'd of liked to see that!"

Tabitha looked at him coldly.

"You infuriate me," she said. "Screaming with laughter, and there's that man outside—"

"He's elsewhere," Asey said. "Him an' me had a brief game of tag—"

"Who was it?" Tabitha and Marian demanded.

"I wouldn't know."

"What?" Tabitha said. "Don't you know?"

"Nope, I seen him loomin' at me out of the hydrangeas, an' I felt his tackle. I felt that plenty. Then I seen him as he went lopin' off into the fog—"

"You mean," Marian said, "you were out there, and you saw him, and still you don't know who that man is?"

"As far as I'm concerned," Asey admitted simply, "he's just an unidentified stranger. Tall, quick, an' male."

Tabitha sniffed.

"I resent that sniff," Asey said. "You wouldn't be sniffin' like that if it'd been you playin' tag with him. He plays hard. Terrible fond of tag, that man is," he added. "Probably that's what he was hangin' around here for. Wanted you two to play with him. He's been tryin' to entice me— look, was he all that scared you, or has there been anything else?"

Tabitha said there had been phone calls.

"That's what I came over to see Marian about, but I've almost forgotten them, with that man trying to get in."

"Phone calls from who?"

"We don't know," Marian said helplessly. "Somebody calls, and when you answer the phone, the person hangs up. Both of us have had them, four or five times. I didn't think anything about the first one, or even the second—"

"But with the third," Tabitha said, "I began to be curious, and then I began to worry a little. Tell him about the Judge, Marian. He had them, too."

"He's on my line," Marian explained. "The phone rang

a lot, but apparently Evan and the Judge were out, so after a while I answered. We often take messages for each other, if we know the other is out. And the same thing happened—when I said hello, there was just a click on the other end."

"Did you ask the girl about it?" Asey wanted to know. "The phone office girl?"

"We've got a new girl," Marian said, "and she's quite formal. You can't call up any more and just ask for Tabitha. She makes you give the number."

"I noticed that," Asey said, "today. She told me to consult the book."

"Well, I asked her if she could tell me who was calling," Marian said, "and she told me that doubtless it was an error, and if I hung up, the party would call again."

"I didn't even ask her," Tabitha said. "Not just because she and I have had words on several occasions, but I didn't want to startle the Abbotts by asking about mysterious phone calls. That's why I drove over to see Marian, and talk with her about them— Asey, what's this all about?"

"I think," Asey said, "someone is tryin' to scare you, an' it looks like he's bein' successful. After all, Tabitha, if that man outside intended to do any harm, he wouldn't have advertised himself. He couldn't have had such awful evil thoughts, or he'd have done more than just push me down hard."

"Why should we be scared?" Marian demanded. "I mean, why should someone want to scare us?"

"Well," Asey said, "there are lots of nice reasons. In the first place, he warned you three to watch out, an' so he's pretty much got to give you somethin' to watch out about. An' he knows you'll report it all to me—he sort of paved the way for that by the first rock he threw at Banbury's house, with the note tellin' me to keep out of things."

"I still don't understand," Tabitha said.

"A magician," Asey said, "chatters an' tells funny stories when he does hard tricks. Or else he tells you just where to watch. These notes, an' these phone calls, they serve about the same purpose. Someone wants to do a little divertin', I think."

"Then why don't they divert the police?" Tabitha demanded. "Why on earth should they divert us—oh, I see. They know we'll tell you, and that'll divert you, I suppose.

Well, I wish they'd stop. I'm getting tired of it— Asey, there have been times today when I've almost been sorry that I was so nice to the Banburys, and made them stay here, for all they've done for the town! Marian, are you going to come home with me, or stay here?"

"You certainly don't think I'm going to stay here alone, do you?" Marian said. "Half an hour in this house by myself and I should be frightened to a pulp. The creakings always bother me, and after tonight, they'd simply slay me. Wait till I get my toothbrush— Asey, did Evan tell you where he'd taken Mrs. Banbury and Jane?"

"Who? Evan Chase?"

"We decided," Tabitha said, "that probably Evan had taken them off somewhere, out of Farley's reach. What does Farley think? Does he know where they are?"

"Farley," Asey said, "sort of suspected that I knew about the Banbury women. Far as that goes, I think he suspects I know about Banbury."

"What do you mean, know about Banbury?" Tabitha asked. "Farley took Phineas up to jail hours and hours ago, everyone knows that."

"Yes," Asey said, "but Phineas left—"

"Left! You mean, he escaped?" Tabitha said anxiously. "He broke jail? Oh, he never did! How terrible! Why should he do that? Why—"

"Why?" Marian broke in. "How did he, Asey? How could he have? What for?"

Both women, Asey thought, looked and sounded pretty much worked up about the whole thing.

"I shouldn't worry about him," Asey said reassuringly. "I sort of toyed with the idea of goin' in for some rescue work, but they've left him an out, up the Cape, an' he'll be bright enough to take it. 'Course, I think he'll be down here sooner or later, but I don't think there's any need of worryin' about him—"

"But it's dangerous for him!" Tabitha said. "They really didn't have any proof against him, before, but breaking jail is a charge he won't be able to get out of—oh, dear! I suppose he's worrying about Lu and Jane—did anything happen that would make him worry about them, Asey?"

"Farley," Asey told her, "tried some psychology, an' it backfired on him. But I wouldn't worry about Phineas."

Tabitha walked over to the window and looked out.

"This fog!" she said. "This infernal fog! I've always said, almost anything in the world seems to happen during a Stayer And it does! Asey, you may not worry about Phineas, but I do. Suppose he gets here—"

"He'll steer clear of Farley. Give him credit, Tabitha. Banbury'll look out. He won't let himself get arrested—"

"I'm not thinking about his being arrested," Tabitha said. "That part doesn't worry me. I'd be glad to see him arrested— Asey, whoever started all this business about Banbury is still on the job. Whoever began the propaganda about him, whoever put the arsenic in the tarts—for that matter, whoever killed Abner. That man's still waiting here. Under the cover of this fog, there's no limit to what he might do. And—"

"Look," Marian said excitedly. "Wait a minute, Tabitha, I've got an idea—you don't suppose those calls could have been from Phineas? Tabitha, could it have been Phineas who was trying to get in?"

"Whatever," Tabitha said, "would make you think that?"

"He'll come right back here, won't he?" Marian said. "Where else would he go? And he'll know that the police will probably be at Banbury Bog. So he won't go there. And he knows there'll be your boarders at your house. He might not want to take the chance of going there, either. So, maybe he would come here— Asey, don't you think so?"

"Of course not!" Tabitha spoke up before Asey had a chance to answer. "Marian, if Phineas Banbury should come here—"

"You've got to admit," Marian interrupted, "that it's a good place for him to come!"

"Yes, maybe it is. But if he should come here, he'd never crawl up a trellis, or poke around trying to find a loose window! He'd march to the front door, and bang the knocker, just as Asey did!"

"He might not," Marian said stoutly. "Perhaps he'd think that was the better way—"

"You mean," Asey suppressed a chuckle, "that Banbury'd think he ought to add breakin' an' enterin' to his crime sheet, now that he's done some breakin' an' leavin'? Sort of to balance things up?"

"You can laugh all you want to," Marian said, "but

that's what I think. And—and I'm going to stay right here, so if Phineas comes back—"

"Alone?" Asey said.

"With no phone?" Tabitha added. "Marian, don't be silly! I can see your point about the possibility of Phineas coming here—but really, Marian, after what you and I have gone through, do you want to stay here alone?"

Marian hesitated.

"There!" Tabitha said. "Now, go get your toothbrush, and come along. If Phineas should come here, I'm sure—"

"I'm going to stay," Marian announced. "Lord knows, I'll be afraid, but—I've got to, Tabitha. I must. If he comes here, he'll need someone. I'm going to stay!" She paused, and then went on in a less defensive tone, "Er—Tabitha, can't you lend me Mary for the night?"

"If you want to ask Mary," Tabitha said, "you may. I certainly shan't urge her to come over here, myself."

"I will. I'll drive over behind you," Marian said, "and then if Mary'll come back and stay with me, she and I will drive back. If she won't—well, let's hope she will."

Asey looked curiously after Mrs. Milton as she went upstairs.

"When she gets an idea," he said, "she certainly hangs on to it, don't she?"

"That was exactly what Abner used to say," Tabitha told him. "But I know how she feels, Asey. Both of us would like to do anything in the world to help Phineas, and I suppose she feels that this is a way. It's no more bizarre than some of the things I've thought of doing, today— All ready, Marian?"

Back at Tabitha's house, Mary reluctantly agreed to spend the night with Marian Milton.

She did not seem to be very keen on the idea, Asey thought. It was a faint display of opposition on the part of Tabitha that finally decided her.

"I'll trail you two over," he said, "if you'd like me to."

Marian looked at him gratefully.

"I should, Asey. And can you think of anything—well, anything that would make a noise, if—if we wanted to attract someone's attention?"

"I know what," Tabitha said. "There's a watchman's rattle up attic. I'll get that—"

Unless Asey was vastly mistaken, Phineas Banbury had just been put ashore from that motor boat which was now chugging back up the inlet and out the bay.

CHAPTER X

at Syl's wharf.

In one motion he swung himself up and secured the little sharpie, and then he started for Pettigrew's landing. He was taking the long way, but it was safer to go by foot. There were plenty of chances to get twisted in a boat, between the "Emily" and Pettigrew's.

Banbury had come back. There was no question about it in Asey's mind. Slick and easy, that was the Banbury way of getting things done. He wouldn't wait for good weather and a plane; he'd hire a boat and go through the fog. And probably, Asey thought, there were still plenty of men around who had made their living running that inlet during prohibition days. Banbury had found an ex-rum runner, and hired him. Making Wellfleet instead of Weesit was a perfectly excusable error, under the circumstances. And Wellfleet would be near enough to Weesit, anyway. Banbury wouldn't have carped over a few miles.

And no one would have come in any inlet on the Cape tonight without plenty of reason. Not unless large checks had been waved around.

Asey had not recognized Banbury's voice, but the first man who called. the man who had awakened Mrs. Banbury, was not the same man who yelled the last time.

In that interval, Asey decided, Banbury had been put ashore.

He paused at the foot of Pettigrew's landing, and listened.

This shore was one place he knew like a book, fog or no fog. And it was all strange territory to Phineas.

This, Asey thought confidently, was where he would nip Brother Banbury in the bud, before he started getting himself in trouble.

But Asey was doomed to disappointment.

Ten minutes of sharp listening brought forth no sound of footsteps, no noise of anyone wandering around, wondering which way to go. There was only the lapping of small waves on the shore and the rush of the tide in the inlet.

"Huh," Asey said, and walked to his car.

He started it, and let the motor run.

Banbury needed a car. If the man was playing possum, that motor turning over ought to bring him out, all right.

When the church clock struck four, Asey gave up and drove toward his own house.

Leaving the car in Briar Lane, he skirted his orchard and approached the back door.

He heard the voices of the men in his driveway long before he saw them, and the name of Farley was clearly audible.

"How to lay an ambush." Asey murmured. "Rule one: Be sure to mention the name of the cop in charge. Rule two: Take a deep breath an' yell it out loud again."

Certainly Banbury would never be trapped!

"Did Farley say to stay?"

"Yeah. Farley said to stay."

"How long?"

"He just said to stay."

Asey turned and started back to his car.

That settled that. Banbury would never linger very long in the vicinity of those yowling cops.

But where would he go?

It had been easy enough, a few hours before, to say that Banbury would come back to Weesit, but which portion of Weesit would he go to? Where would he go?

Asey asked himself that question several times, and gave himself a different answer each time.

Banbury Bog itself was the logical place, but Phineas would know that Farley would be expecting him to go there to see Mrs. Banbury and Jane. On the other hand, Phineas Banbury was perfectly capable of marching there. He seemed to prefer the most direct method of doing things.

He might go to Tabitha Sparrow's. But arousing Tabitha would mean arousing her boarders, too, and that would be bad all around. Particularly, Asey thought, after that watchman's rattle.

That left Marian Milton's and Judge Chase's.

There were many more reasons for his going to see the Judge, in view of this jail-breaking episode.

But there was always the other side. Judge Chase was an uncommonly just man. It was possible that he might feel it was his duty to return Banbury to jail, or to the police.

Maybe, Asey thought as he started the car, maybe Marian Milton's ideas hadn't been so foolish as they sounded at first. There would be no police lurking around her house. There would be no boarders to be aroused. And Banbury probably knew well enough that she would do anything he asked.

"Milton wins," Asey said, and turned the car back toward Weesit.

Once again he took the old lane, and stepped out among the marigolds.

How Banbury might have got there without any visible means of transportation, Asey didn't know. But it was time for milk trucks to be rolling about, and Banbury probably could hook a ride, somehow. He wouldn't let those few miles thwart him.

Asey made a careful inspection of the old Knowles place. There was no one up, no one stirring, no sign of life whatsoever.

Asey eyed the trellis.

At the top, he listened to the snores issuing from the bedroom, and then he climbed down.

Banbury hadn't arrived.

Back in his car, among the marigolds, Asey suddenly hit on the solution.

"Cummings!" he said. "That's where he went an' headed for, the doc's. He liked the doc, an' there's a place where he could find out everything, without any bother of. cops hangin' around—"

He really let the car out, returning to Wellfleet.

At the doctor's house, he put his finger on the night bell and held it there.

A window opened above him.

"Yes? Who's there?"

"Asey, Mrs. Cummings—where's the doc? Ain't he here?"

"He's at Cranberry Bog."

"You mean, Banbury Bog?"

"Banbury or Cranberry, whatever they call Bog House these days. That's where he is. Detained, they told me over the phone."

"Oho," Asey said. "Did Farley detain him?"

"He might have," Mrs. Cummings said, "but if you ask me, I'd say it was Mrs. Bemis."

"Mrs. Who?" Asey was thoroughly confused.

"The doctor can't stand her," Mrs. Cummings said. "He says she makes him speechless. The Bemises were coming over for bridge. If you ask me, that's why he was detained, and when he comes home, I'm going to give him a good piece of my mind, that's what!"

Asey grinned. Mrs. Cummings was always distributing good pieces of her mind about, gratis, and sometimes he wondered how the woman managed to have any mind left.

"Asey—you still there? Well, tell me, Asey, isn't that Cranberry in jail? I thought they'd arrested Cranberry."

"You mean Banbury?"

"Whatever his name is. When'd he get out of jail?"

Asey swallowed.

"Has Cr—I mean, has Banbury been here?" he asked. "He has. I see—look, I'm gettin' a crick in my neck here, Mrs. Cummings. Could you let me in? I'd sort of like to know about Banbury."

Mrs. Cummings said, not too graciously, that she'd let him in if he waited until she got something on. She also muttered something about the occupation of the next husband she had. Asey couldn't tell whether she said bricklayer or brickmaker, but it was clear that Mrs. Cummings was weary of the medical profession and its ramifications.

She was still muttering when she opened the door for him.

"No sleep," she said, "not one good night's sleep in thirty years, and even if we take a little trip somewhere, there's always some woman having a baby in the upper berth across the aisle. Come in, Asey. I know I shouldn't splutter so, but sometimes I just can't help it. You're the fourth person that's got me out of bed tonight—gracious, it's almost morning! And not counting the milkman, either. I'm going to write a letter to the milk company and give them a piece of my mind. That new man's the noisiest they ever had. Is there anything the matter with you, Asey?"

Asey grinned.

"I ain't sure," he said. "I wasn't this confused when I come here."

"Well, there's nothing the matter with you, is there? Nothing I've got to bind up for *you?*"

"No, I'm whole—say, tell me, who you been havin' to bind up?" Asey had an uncomfortable feeling that it might have been Banbury.

"Oh, Mrs. Spalding, her knee slipped out again, but I've bound it up before. And then Evan Chase. Just those two, but that was enough."

"What's wrong with Evan?"

"He had this burn on the side of his neck—it wasn't such a bad burn," Mrs. Cummings said, "but it pained him a lot. But I fixed him up. He said he'd been poking a clinker out of the kitchen stove grate, when the tea kettle tipped over and scalded him—"

"What!"

"That's what he said. I didn't understand how it could have happened, either. I told him I didn't see how any living man who was poking a clinker could manage to have a tea kettle tip over on him, unless he did it on purpose to get me out of bed. So—"

"So he was scalded, was he?" Asey said. "Not burned, but scalded by boilin' water—"

"Well, scalded *or* burned, whatever you want to call it," Mrs. Cummings said, "he got me out of bed. And I still don't see how it could have happened, do you?"

"No," Asey said, "I don't. Say." he added, "what does Evan Chase look like? I don't think I've seen him since he was a kid in school."

"Oh, he's tall, and he's got that Chase look around the mouth, and brown eyes—he's not bad looking."

"Active sort of feller?" Asey inquired.

"He certainly is. Always playing tennis or golf, or swimming—the doctor told him he ought to slow up, or he'd have real trouble with his bad ankle. He hurt it playing football in college, and the doctor says he's never favored it enough—"

Asey barely listened as Mrs. Cummings continued to chatter on about Evan Chase. He had learned what he wanted to know.

Evan Chase was tall, and he was active, and he had played football.

And he had been scalded.

And, not so very long ago, Marian Milton and Tabitha had tossed boiling water on the tall, active man who had climbed up the trellis at Marian's. That same tall, active man who had jolted Asey with that straight-arm.

That, Asey thought, was an item that was worth delaying his search for Banbury for.

"What about Banbury?" Asey asked as Mrs. Cummings paused for breath. "You said there was nothin' the matter with him. What did he come here for?"

"I'm sure I don't know," Mrs. Cummings returned. "If I'd known him, I'd have given him a good piece of my mind for coming here and waking me up for nothing. The way he rang that bell! I just thought he'd never stop!"

"When did he come?"

"It was just after that noisy milkman rattled up," Mrs. Cummings told him. "And he rang, and he rang, and finally he stopped long enough so I could ask what he wanted, and he wanted the doctor, and I told him the doctor was over at Cranberry Bog—"

"Banbury Bog—"

"Well, you know what I mean!" Mrs. Cummings said impatiently. "Why couldn't they just have kept on calling that place Bog House, I wonder? Anyway, I asked who it was, and if anyone was sick, and he said that he was Banbury, and I thought he said Cranberry, and we had an awful time straightening that out, Asey. An awful time!"

Asey had a beautiful mental picture of the scene, with Mrs. Cummings Cranberrying from the upstairs window, and Banbury Banburying, with a crick in his neck, from the doorstep.

"Finally, he asked me if there was anyone sick at Banbury Bog," Mrs. Cummings said, "and I told him not that I knew of, and he asked if I was sure, and I said yes. Then he thanked me and went off. I don't know what he came here for if he wasn't sick, and I don't understand what he was doing here, anyway. They told me he was up in jail."

"So he just thanked you and went," Asey said. "Huh. Where'd he go?"

"I don't know. I got back into my bed. And just as my head touched the pillow, that milkman came back. He goes all the way out to Thatchers', after he comes here, and then he stops on the way back from Thatchers' and dumps his empties at the corner. And how he did dump! Slam, bang, biff, slam, bang! And then just as I got back to sleep again, you came along!"

Asey nodded.

Banbury had come in the milk truck, and he had left by it.

"How long ago was Banbury here?" he asked.

"Three-quarters of an hour or more. Yes, almost an hour. Asey, I thought he was arrested, and up in jail!"

"He was," Asey said. "Huh. I s'pose I could go chasin' milk trucks, but it seems to me I wouldn't get far—didn't he say a word where he was goin'?"

"Not a word. Asey, what's the matter? Why are you so interested in him?"

Asey reminded her that there had been a murder.

"Abner Grove. Yes, I know, of course I know that!" Mrs. Cummings said. "Everyone knows. It doesn't seem to me that anyone talked of anything else, all day yesterday. Gracious, we even talked about it all last evening, the Bemises and I—we couldn't get a fourth, it was so late when they phoned about the doctor's being detained."

"What did you think about it all?" Asey asked.

He really didn't care two cents what Mrs. Cummings thought. He merely wanted to keep her occupied while he did some thinking, himself.

But Mrs. Cummings was beginning to hit her conversational stride. She discussed the murder of Abner Grove at such length and with such emphasis that Asey couldn't ignore her.

"Ed Bemis said, when a man came into a town the way Cranberry—I mean, Banbury, did he was bound to step on someone's toes, and make someone mad. But as Dora and I said, whose toes could he step on? You know yourself, Asey, there isn't anyone at all important over in Weesit! Over here, or in Orleans, there might have been. But not Weesit!"

Her tone implied that Weesit was a sort of slum, inhabited by a very low grade type of person.

"I don't know," Asey said, "there's plenty of good people over there, I think—"

"Well, as Dora and I said, who! Who, when you stop and think it out? There's Judge Chase, I'll grant you. But you couldn't step on his toes by helping the town. He doesn't think there's any place in the world like Weesit. And he's the only important man. Of course, if you count women, there's Tabitha Sparrow and Marian Milton—"

"Yes," Asey said wearily, "there always seems to be them two!"

"But they're women!" Mrs. Cummings said. "Don't you see? That's what Dora and I told Ed. They're women! And did that faze Ed Bemis? It did not. He said, that with her tweed coats and her man's collars, Marian Milton was as good as any man, any day. And he said, as far as business ability went, he'd back Tabitha against all comers. But as Dora and I said, you can't get away from the fact that they're women, and it was a man— Asey, I do believe there's someone else coming here! Oh, dear, cars!"

Asey walked to the window and pulled aside the curtain.

A police car and the doctor's sedan were drawn up in front of the house.

"Mrs. Cummings," Asey said hurriedly, "will you do just what I say? Don't mention Banbury. Don't let on he was here. No matter what anyone says, don't mention Banbury. You won't, will you?"

"Why not?"

"Here's Farley, with the doc," Asey said. "You can't tell what Farley might think. He might think you was mixed up in things—"

"Me? Why should he—"

"Listen," Asey said desperately, "I wasn't goin' to tell you, but they think the doc might have been—uh—the person who got the arsenic that got put in the tarts."

That, he thought, would hold Mrs. Cummings, and it did.

She just sat back in her chair and watched as Dr. Cummings and Farley came in.

It seemed to Asey that Farley had a haunted look about him. Cummings, on the other hand, was curiously placid.

"You, huh?" Farley said.

"I told you there'd be someone!" Cummings said. "I've kept telling you, there'd be someone here, waiting for me— Asey, is it that indigestion again?"

Asey began to understand the haunted look. The doc, he decided, had been spending a happy night driving Farley mad.

"It was awful bad," he said gravely. "Honest, doc, it was awful. But your wife fixed me up. She's spent the whole night fixin' people up."

"I don't," Farley said, "believe one word of it!"

Asey sighed.

"You're an awful suspicious sort of man," he said.

Farley walked over and stood directly in front of Asey.

"Ah!" Cummings said. "You're being confronted, Asey! I've been telling Farley about confronting—in fact, I've been trying to teach him the proper language. Like scouring, as of vicinities. 'We scoured the bog.' And racing. 'We raced to the doctor's office despite the fog, in a high powered police car.' And confronting—that's a pretty good confront, Farley. If you'd just move a little—just a hair's breadth to the right, you'd have as good a confront as I ever saw. You—"

"Will you," Farley said, "shut up?"

"Gladly. Willingly. It just seems to me I've borne the burden of the conversation for a long, long while," the doctor sat down, "and I'm perfectly willing to take a rest. My throat's sore."

"Asey," Farley said, "can you truthfully say that you haven't seen Phineas Banbury tonight? Or this morning?"

"On my word of honor," Asey said. "I haven't seen him since night before last, just after him an' me found Grove."

"You don't know where he is?"

"I don't, Farley. An'," Asey added feelingly, "I hunted. I've hunted plenty!"

"I told you so, Farley," Dr. Cummings said. "I told you so!"

Farley looked at the doctor, and breathed heavily.

"I did," Cummings said. "I told you. I said, I thought that the entire Banbury family had doubtless fled the country for some distant, far-off land— Farley, a police officer should never lose his temper. That's bad. And—oh, no! Never even lunge at a man who's wearing glasses, Farley. That's much worse—"

Muttering things, Farley left.

Dr. Cummings listened appreciatively to the sound of his departing car.

"I don't suppose," he said, "it's really sporting to rile a man who riles as easily as he does, but I must say, I've spent a very enjoyable night. I just let myself go at the expense of the police. I think, from now on, it's going to be wise for me to mind the traffic rules—"

"What's gone on?" Asey asked. "Has anything turned up?"

Cummings started to laugh.

"A cranberry scoop," he said.

"Banbury," Mrs. Cummings said, speaking for the first time. "Banbury."

"Banbury nothing!" he husband said. "A cranberry scoop. What do you mean, Banbury scoop?"

Mrs. Cummings sighed. "I still think it would have been better," she said plaintively, "if they'd just kept on calling it Bog House."

Cummings looked at her anxiously. "Do you feel all right, dear?" he said. "You haven't got that dizzy feeling again, have you?"

"I'm perfectly all right," Mrs. Cummings said, "but every time I've said Cranberry, Asey's corrected me and made me say Banbury—"

"What about the scoop?" Asey asked.

"Well, Farley's had his men running around the bog—"

"What *for?*" Asey asked. "What *for?*"

"Oh, they're scouring it," Cummings said. "I couldn't find out why. I suppose they have to do something, so they might as well scour. Well, I got bored a few hours ago—"

"Are you hungry?" his wife asked.

"No, I had them feed me. They opened up some cans of Banbury's—"

"There!" Mrs. Cummings said with satisfaction. "You mean cranberries! Not cans of Banburys, cans of cranberries—"

"I mean," Cummings said, "they opened up some cans of Banbury's. Cans which belonged to Banbury. For God's sakes, what do you think, d'you think they fed me cranberry sauce from a can in the middle of the night?"

"Well, you said—"

"Listen," Asey said. "This scoop."

"Oh, yes. Well, I got bored, so I pestered Farley into going down to the bog and taking me along. And there were those poor dubs, wandering around the bog in the fog—what did you say, dear?"

"Nothing," Mrs. Cummings said. "Bog in the fog!"

"Well, there they were, scouring. Asey, if it ever entered your head to scour the bog, you needn't. They've scoured that bog for all time. So I sat there under a tree by the side of the bog, and watched the flashlights, and listened to the curses, and administered a little first aid to one man that got a thorn in his finger, and then I looked up into this old apple tree I was sitting under, and there was the cranberry scoop, see?"

"No," Asey said. "I don't."

"Why, here was this scoop, stuck up in the crotch of the tree above me. So I climbed up and got the scoop, and took it down, and then I decided to have a little fun with the boys, so I wandered out and dumped it on the bog, and then I maneuvered Farley around till he and I found it again."

"I forget," Asey said, "the penalty for obstructin' justice. Twenty years, I think."

"Pooh! That scoop gave those men more pleasure than anything you could imagine, Asey! They all crowded around and pawed it and asked questions about it, and that fellow with the bat-ears that's some kind of expert, he wanted to know if it was to dig clams with. So I explained the use of a cranberry scoop to him, how those wooden teeth, those wooden finger things—"

"Those what?" Asey said.

"Those teeth, you know. On the bottom. I told him how those wooden teeth scooped up the berries—"

"Wait a sec," Asey said. "Describe the scoop, will you, doc?"

"You know what a cranberry scoop looks like, man alive! You've seen millions of cranberry scoops! Why should I describe a cranberry scoop for you?"

"I just wish," Asey said, "that you would."

"Well, it was about so long," Cummings held his hands about two and a half feet apart, "and about—oh, a foot wide, or so, and it had a handle here—"

"Where?"

"Here." Cummings' forefinger described a little arc in midair. "Right here. On the top."

"On the top. Go on."

"Well, that's all! It was like a box on three sides, and part of the fourth, and the rest of the fourth side had those wooden finger things. Those teeth. Like thick wooden knitting needles. Sort of polished wood. And I wish you'd stop grinning, Asey! I must say, a cranberry scoop is nothing a man can describe with any great amount of ease and fluency! Anyway, I told the expert all about it. He came from Florida, by the way. And he thought it was very significant."

Cummings rocked with silent laughter.

"I think that was mean," his wife said. "Poor man, probably he doesn't know the first thing about cranberry bogs and cranberry scoops. You were mean!"

"You may think it was mean, but the expert thought I'd uncovered the most significant thing he'd ever seen. The fact that the berries on the bog weren't ready to be scooped didn't bother him at all. 'That's significant,' says he—"

Cummings sat up suddenly in his chair, and the smile departed from his face as though someone had wiped it off with a towel.

"Asey," he said sharply, "what is it? Good God, man, you don't think it's significant, too, do you?"

"Considerin'," Asey said, "that there ain't no ripe berries to scoop, yet, an' considerin' it was up in the top of the apple tree—"

"Well, what of that? Probably someone just kept the scoop there!"

"You don't keep scoops up in the top of apple trees," Asey said. "An' besides, doc, you ain't described a real scoop. You just described one of them imitation scoops they sell to tourists in Gifty Shoppeys. You keep magazines in 'em. Yup, under the circumstances, doc, I'm inclined to agree with the bat-eared expert. I think you got something significant there."

CHAPTER XI

"ASEY, YOU'RE JOKING. YOU
think I shouldn't have done that. You're just joking to get
me worked up!"

Asey shook his head.

"I'm not jokin'. I mean it. I think it's significant."

Dr. Cummings' snort of derision could have been heard
in the next town.

"In the name of all that's reasonable, and logical, and
sensible, why should that damn scoop be significant? What
could it signify? No, let me go on, Asey Mayo! Do you
realize, that bat-eared dumbbell began by thinking that
the scoop had something to do with the digging of clams?
He didn't even know what it was. And when I told him,
he was so chagrined at his ignorance that he had to save
his face. So he pretended he'd thought it was significant
all along, all the time, and bore it off in triumph as a clew.
Have you got that?"

"I've no doubt," Mrs. Cummings said, "that the Thatchers have it, too. Must you shout so—and don't knock that
beefsteak plant over again, please! Don't wave your arms
around there. Wave them on this side—"

"Have you got that?" Cummings continued to wave his
arms in all directions. "He thought it was a real scoop, and
he said it was significant. Now, you say it's an imitation
scoop, and you say it's significant. Why?" he wound up
abruptly.

"Because—"Asey began.

But Cummings had got his breath.

suggested. "Never can tell when you might light on another scoop—that a mail box out front there? I never noticed that before."

"It's been there," the doctor said, "since I was a small boy. No mail's been left there for years. I can't think why I don't have the thing removed. But it's a sort of senti- mental landmark, and my patients love it. They leave little notes there, saying things they don't like to say in person, and they leave items there that they'd rather not bring up the front walk. But there hasn't been any actual mail there for years— Asey, did you know they've stopped the trains? The schedules are all shot to hell."

Asey nodded.

"Betsey Porter told Bill and me they was going to stop, the day we got home. Betsey says the social life's got awful disorganized, with no trains to wait for, or no—doc, let's take a peek in your box. Banbury wouldn't know about the mail system. An' there certainly's no better place to leave a note."

There was one there, addressed to Cummings.

Asey passed the envelope over to him.

"You're psychic," the doctor said. "That letter box is the last place I'd ever look for a letter— How did you guess?"

"Banbury," Asey told him, "takes the direct way. Let's go in the house and read it—"

The letter was written on the jail's own official note- paper, a fact which charmed the doctor.

"An' before I go," Asey murmured, "just gimme a couple sheets of your paper, will you? That's a gesture, ain't it? What's he say?"

" 'Going to Weesit,' " Cummings read the firm, flowing script.

"Might as well say he was going to the moon," Asey commented. "That all?"

" 'To see a friend—' "

"Who?"

"He doesn't say. Just a friend. 'Tell them'—I suppose he means his family, doesn't he? 'Tell them not to worry, I am going to settle everything. Tell Asey I will be all right and not to interfere. I have thought everything over and know just what I am doing.' That's all there is."

"Huh," Asey said, "if he knows what he's doin', more

power to him. I'll give him credit, he's got here an' set to work as slick an' easy as anybody could. Funny thing, most business men seem to be plumb dumb fools outside of their own line, but not Banbury. He can run a tart business, or a town, or an escape from jail, it's all the same to him. Well, I'll stop thinkin' about him, if he's so cocksure. I just hope he don't come to no grief."

"I'd forget him entirely," Cummings said. "After all, if he's escaped your clutches, he can keep out of Farley's —oh, did I tell you about the reporters? They asked about you, and Farley said you'd just come back from a cruise with your millionaire friend, Bill Porter, and hadn't got back into harness yet, but that you concurred with the opinion expressed by the police. I pretended to swallow that, and then I said, 'Farley, are you trying to make Asey out to be a dirty capitalist, or are you just trying to ruin his reputation?' He could have shot me. Yes, I've got to mind my traffic habits. He'll have every state cop laying for me. Asey, what's this person hunting with the scoop, something small?"

"As a rule," Asey said, "you're not apt to lose large things—"

"Not at all, I lost a car in Boston once. I thought I'd left it on a street, but I'd parked it on the tenth floor of a garage. I—"

"Just absent-minded, that's you," Asey said. "Well, I don't think anyone's lost a car, or he wouldn't be huntin' so hard through the pigeon holes of Abner Grove's desk, as he did today—no, it's tomorrow, isn't it?"

"It's Friday," Cummings said. "Hm. Something small, portable—hard, too, I suppose. Something those wooden finger things wouldn't hurt. Got any thoughts?"

"Yup," Asey said. "My final guess on that is Abner Grove's watch. His favorite watch, that Banbury give him for being a nice selectman."

Cummings thought for a moment.

"Why would anyone hunt that? Why would it matter where it was found, or who found it? In the house or in the bog—what of it? Why?"

"Someone's huntin' somethin' small an' hard an' portable," Asey said, "an' Abner's watch measures up to them standards. Besides, the Banburys said he always had it. Jane told you herself about that."

"But why?" Cummings persisted.

Asey shrugged. "But it's important enough for someone to hunt, pretty thorough. This bog scoopin' proves that."

"I shall never lose sight of the fact," Cummings said, "that I am responsible for that scoop. Asey, the police have never got off that bog, but you don't think he was killed there, do you?"

Asey told him about the cane whose head Tabitha had sawed off, and about the tubs by the oyster shell walk.

"That works out, you see," Asey said. "An' then Grove was expectin' someone. Someone he knew, an' wouldn't be too formal with—there wasn't anythin' formal about that old suit he had on. The person came, an' as he left, goin' down the oyster shell path, he biffed Abner—"

"Who fell into the tub of cistern water—"

"Yup. An' he biffed with Banbury's cane, which the Banbury women don't know where they saw last. Seems everyone gives Banbury a cane."

Cummings shouted with laughter.

"I thought it was funny, too," Asey said, and explained what Tabitha had told him about its being the Judge's suggestion. "An' then Jane said everyone give him canes. Well, where was I? Oh. Person comes back later, havin' rushed away after biffin' Abner, an' finds Abner drowned. Puts him in convenient Welcome Wagon—an' so on. Before leavin', lays out food, so as to make interested parties feel that Abner was interrupted in the middle of gettin' supper. Now, I want to go to Weesit an'—"

"Wait," Cummings said. "Just a couple more items I want to have cleared up in my mind. In the process of killing Abner, or moving him to the bog, or even before, his watch became lost. Right? And someone wants the watch, and is hunting like hell for it, so it must be a vital factor, but you wouldn't know why. Right? Now, the possession of Banbury's cane means that the person had thought all this out well in advance, doesn't it? Right. And—this occurred to me tonight. When were you and Bill Porter supposed to return from your cruise—wasn't it after Labor Day?"

"We planned, originally," Asey said, "to get back three weeks from tomorrow. Then Bill got into a sweat about his new models, and ripped back—"

"There, see?" Cummings said. "You wouldn't have been here, would you? Did you think of that?"

Asey shook his head.

"No, I hadn't, but it casts a sort of light on that little suggestion that Jane found on her rock, about my stayin' out. Huh. I wonder."

"I bet," Cummings said, "you'll find a place where someone planned for you to be away. Something they knew you might notice, but no one else would. I'll bet you'll find a slip-up, somewhere. No, wait. One more thing. Have you found out whose toes Banbury stepped hardest on?"

Asey sighed.

"I'm just a little sick," he said, "of them stepped-on toes. The consensus is they belong to three folks. Tabitha, Marian Milton an' Judge Chase—"

"Your delegation?"

"Yup."

"Well," Cummings said, "the revolution against Banbury would have started with the upper classes. What do you think about it all?"

"Old Mr. Abbott alibied Tabitha. Mary alibied Marian Milton."

"I'd never suspect either of 'em. Never Tabitha, under any circumstances. Never Marian, after that day she fainted in my office, just because of a little dripping blood. I was cutting a fish hook out of her hand."

"What about the Judge?"

"He's a bit old," Cummings said, "for active villainy, don't you think? He's well over seventy. On the other hand, he's tough and wiry, and he brags about never having had a tooth filled, and he takes a cold bath every morning. And he can down a supper of Cape Cod barefoot laced with pork scraps, and topped off with Huckleberry Slump, and then he can sit at his desk and work on the history of Weesit with a clear mind and an untroubled stomach. Me, I'd be in the hospital. He's a pompous old duffer, but he loves Weesit, and it's always seemed to me he welcomed Banbury and what Banbury did. He's talked with me about it."

"So you cross him off?"

"Yes, certainly! Hell," Cummings said, "it's probably some dish washer over at the Inn who feels he's not getting enough wages, or some thwarted quohaugger, or someone like that!"

"No one," Asey said tentatively, "has ever thought of Evan Chase."

"Good God, why should they think of Evan? He's not a native—well, in a way. But not really. He did a lot of work for Banbury, and at Bog House, but he had plenty of work before he came here. He has an office in Boston. Say, now I think of it, I've heard a lot of talk about Jane Banbury and Evan— It's odd he hasn't been around to find her, or see you."

"He's been around," Asey said. "I didn't see him, but he was here, to consult you professionally. He'd got scalded an' your wife fixed him up."

"Scalded? How?"

"He said," Asey drawled a little, "that the tea kettle got up on its hind legs an' tipped."

"But," Cummings said. "But what? Go on. I know there's a but. I know your but voice."

"But I'm inclined to wonder," Asey said, "if he didn't meet that boilin' water on his way up Marian Milton's trellis."

Cummings stared at him. "What!"

Asey explained about his trip to Mrs. Milton's, the man who had tackled him, and all the rest.

"Good God!" Cummings said excitedly. "What are you waiting for? I could see the Judge's brain working in this —your lack of proof, your lack of clews! No weapon. All this planning. But after all, he's well over seventy! But— don't you see, Asey? The Judge planned it, and Evan did it! Asey, why wait? Why don't you start right out? Why didn't you start right out, at once?"

"I'm goin' to give Evan," Asey said, "enough rope—"

Mrs. Cummings came hurriedly into the room, and beckoned to them.

Without saying a word, she led Asey and the doctor to the front steps, and pointed to the battered, bleeding figure lying there.

CHAPTER XII

DR. CUMMINGS DID NOT at first recognize the man.

Then he turned to Asey.

"Rope," he said, "is just about the only thing that hasn't been given him—"

"You mean, that's Evan Chase?" Asey stared down at the huddled figure on the steps. "That's Evan, there?"

"It certainly is," Cummings said, "and someone's done a job on him. Help me get him in, and I'll get to work—"

"Is he alive?" Mrs. Cummings asked, as the two men lifted Evan and carried him into the doctor's office. "Is he alive? What's happened to him?"

"Uh, he's heavy," Cummings said. "Ease him around, Asey—that's right. Hot water, Nettie, quick. Sure, he's alive."

"He looks dead to me," Mrs. Cummings said. "All that blood! And look at his eye—what happened to his eye?"

"The tea kettle bit him," Cummings said, and gave her a little push. "Nettie, get that water—"

"But his nose! Look at it! What—oh, all right! I'll get your water—but don't let him bleed on the carpet! I'm so tired of having that carpet cleaned! Oh, the poor boy— do something about him, you two! He looks terrible!"

While Cummings bustled about the office, Asey surveyed the figure of Evan Chase.

"Those," he said, "are what I call contusions an'

abrasions received as a result of an extensive assault an'
battery. What's your diagnosis?"

"You're in my way," Cummings said. "Move over there
and get his coat off. Hm. There's sort of a touch of may-
hem about this, isn't there—good God, he's bunged up!
He's lost a tooth—"

Mrs. Cummings came in with a kettle of water.

"Here," she said. "Now, give me that cotton and let me
help before that carpet gets ruined—oh, his poor face!"

"He's coming to," the doctor said. "He—what's that?"

"Something about his uncle—gracious!" Mrs. Cummings
said, "You don't suppose Judge Chase gave him that eye,
and that nose, and knocked his tooth out, do you?"

"No!" Evan said, and passed out of the picture again.

Half an hour later, Evan reassured them that his uncle
had done no such thing.

Swathed in bandages, and propped up on the doctor's
operating table, he asked for a cigarette. After several ex-
perimental gropings, he found a corner of his mouth which
seemed capable of holding the one which Asey lighted for
him.

"Uncle's against capital punishment—ow! I can't manage words that size. No, it wasn't uncle—what gave you
that idea?"

"Who is responsible?" Asey asked. "Or were you just
run over by a steam roller?"

"This," Evan said, "is the work of one Phineas Banbury."

"What!"

Evan nodded.

"When?" Asey demanded.

"Around five." Evan felt his mouth. "Did he knock out
my bridge? He must have. I sound queer. Yes, Banbury
at five."

"Where?"

"Outside our house. He came charging out of the fog
like a wolf on the fold, and started banging our knocker—"

"How'd he get there?"

Evan shook his head. "I don't know. He came just after
the milkman came, and banged our knocker—"

"Just a sec," Asey said, "what were you doin' outside
your house around five—waitin' to tell the milkman to
leave an extra quart?"

"I was taking one more look around before I went to bed," Evan said.

"One more look for *what?* For heaven's sakes," Cummings said, "get on with your story. This is worse than having hairs yanked out by a tweezer! One more look for what? For who? Get on—"

"Don't bully that poor boy so!" Mrs. Cummings said. "It's all he can do to talk, poor thing, with his lips all swelled and split, and his tooth gone, and his bridge knocked out!"

"We feel for the poor boy's condition," Cummings retorted, "but the poor boy's still got a lot of explaining to do, hasn't he, Asey?"

"I'm 'fraid you have, Evan," Asey said. "Who was you taking looks around for?"

"I don't know," Evan said.

He watched the expression that flitted over Asey's face.

"Maybe," he went on, "maybe I shouldn't have come here. I knew you'd never believe me. I know just what you're thinking. You think I walked into a door handle, and then threw a few bricks at myself, and then came over here and collapsed artistically—ow! on the doorstep. Well, I didn't. If you think this is an act, you're crazy!"

"To tell you the truth," Asey said, "that thought never occurred to me. There are limits to the damages a man can do to himself. But let's get back. You was waitin' around outside your house at five, for someone. But you don't know who. Can you enlarge on that part?"

Evan drew a long breath.

"Is there anything, first, that you can do about this taste in my mouth, doctor? No? Well, give me another cigarette. Asey, this all begins on Wednesday night. Night before last. Night of that damn church supper. I'd spent the day in Boston. It was a scorcher there, so I waited till evening to drive down, and I got home around midnight. Uncle was waiting up for me, and he told me about those damn poisoned tarts. I wanted to go right over to the Banburys at once, but he wouldn't let me—"

"Why not?" Asey asked.

"He seemed terribly worried, Asey. Terribly upset. He said it would be best if I stayed home. I didn't want to get him any more worked up, so I said all right, I would. I went up to my room—and d'you know what he did? He came along a few minutes later, and he locked me in!"

"What did you do?" Asey said.

"Went out the window on a sheet, just like a girl in boarding school. That was what I intended to do in the first place, anyway. But there was uncle at the bottom." Evan managed a wry smile. "We both laughed. I'd slid out that window plenty of times when I was a kid, and uncle was always waiting for me at the bottom. He asked me to go back. He said, 'I mean this, Evan. I know it will be best if you do. You can go see them in the morning.' So, I went back to bed, and stayed there."

"An' what did the Judge do?"

"He went to bed, too. Then, in the morning, Tabitha and Marian came rushing over and told us about Abner Grove, and they decided they'd better go for you, at once. I thought that was a good idea, and I said I'd drive them all over, but uncle made some excuse, and took me out in the back sitting room, and said he wanted me to stay home. He said there was no need of my going over to see you, Asey, and that he didn't want me to go to Banbury's, either. I said that Jane and her mother would probably be wondering where I was, but he was adamant."

"Why?" Cummings asked. "Did he give you any reason?"

"No, doctor, he didn't. We got pretty mad at each other, and then uncle's voice broke, and he started talking about the honor of Weesit, and the honor of the Chases, and the late, great judge—well, there wasn't anything I could do but give my word of honor not to leave the house. Uncle's a swell old fellow, and—oh, you know. So I champed around the house while he and Tab and Marian came to see you, Asey. I couldn't get Jane on the phone— some cop said she was busy. And—well, by the time he came back from your place, I was mad. We had a lot more words about Weesit and the Chase family, and then I finally slammed out of the house and went to the Banburys'—"

"To Banbury Bog?" Asey asked.

"Yes, but the cops wouldn't let me in. Then I went to Abner's—I thought you might possibly be there. But I didn't see your car, so I turned at the bend and came back to town and tried to find out what had happened anyway. Then I went back to the bog, and found Jane and her mother were gone, and they'd arrested Phineas—"

Asey gave him another cigarette.

"Had quite a time, didn't you?"

"I did," Evan said. "Funny, this doesn't taste like a cigarette, either. Well, all that business of Abner, and Phineas arrested, and Jane and her mother gone—that was the least of my worries, Asey. Then uncle began. And the fog came in."

"Uncle began what?" Cummings wanted to know. "And where does this get to Banbury, at five o'clock this morning? When—"

"Let Asey go on," Mrs. Cummings said severly. "Let Evan go on. Don't fret so!"

"Uncle began," Evan said, "to act up. When I went back to the house, Alma said he hadn't been home for lunch, and I began to get a little worried. And then the phone began to ring, and when I answered, there was just the click of someone hanging up on the other end. That bothered me. But when uncle didn't come home for supper, I got good and worried, and went out and hunted for him. Where do you suppose he was, Asey?"

"My guess," Asey said, "is on Banbury's cranberry bog."

Mrs. Cummings made a little exclamation.

"How did you know?" Evan demanded. "That's just where he was. I grabbed him just before a fresh relay of cops came, and yanked him home. My God, you know what the police would have thought at that point, if they found him wandering around the bog—"

"I know," the doctor observed crisply, "what I think."

"I told him," Evan said, "that I didn't think the scene of a murder was any place for him, and that seemed to subdue him. He said he'd just had an idea, and he was carrying it out, and it never occurred to him what anyone would think. He seemed awfully tired, and after supper, I suggested that he lie down, and he said he guessed he'd go to bed—"

"Are you breakin' it to us gentle," Asey said, "that he foxed you, an' went out?"

"That's just what he did!"

"Not down a sheet from the window, I trust!" Cummings said.

Evan nodded.

"He did. You see, I'd locked his door, so he went out the window. By the grace of God, I got him out by the phone pole at the end of the lane, where he'd stopped to get his bearings in the fog, and I tell you, I marched him back to the house! And then," Evan said with satisfaction, "I told him a few things about the honor of the Chases, for a change!"

Asey played with his pipe.

"Did you find out what the Judge's idea was, Evan?"

"Asey, I asked that man questions till I was hoarse. I cross-questioned him, and yelled at him, and wagged my finger under his nose, and I got just exactly nowhere at all! Then I took another tack, and asked if there wasn't something *I* could do. And he said, all he wanted me to do was to keep out of this. Then I said I'd call you, Asey. I said if he had any ideas about this Abner Grove business, you were the person to know 'em. And he said, in effect, that this was something he could attend to better than you could."

"Did you get the impression," Asey asked, "that he was huntin' somethin'?"

"I did at first," Evan said. "I thought at first that he'd thought of something that might be a clew, and was hunting it. Then I thought it over, and I began to feel there was more to it than that. He had sort of taken to looking out of the window, nervously, and he listened for noises. And then there was the way he acted about me, about not wanting me to get mixed up in anything. That's just what he'd do if there was danger of any sort."

"But would he go out hunting danger, if he thought there was any?" Cummings said.

"If uncle," Evan said, "thinks that the honor of Weesit and the Chase family depends on his finding something out about this murder, you can be sure he'd never think of danger. Never."

Asey agreed. "I think you're right there. Huh. So he wouldn't tell you anythin', an' he wouldn't let you tackle anythin'—"

"He wouldn't even promise me to stay put," Evan said. "But I solved that one. I locked him up. He's safe. This time, he'll stay put. I know, because I used to get an occasional dose of that closet, myself, in the old days. I put an easy chair in the old eaves closet, and brought up a bridge lamp, and his pipe, and his manuscript, and he's locked and bolted in there. And—"

"The poor man!" Mrs. Cummings said. "Locked in a closet! Why, he'll smother—"

"Oh, no, he won't! There's a window about six inches square," Evan said, "and he can slide that open. But he can't get out of it. I couldn't get out of it at the age of seven. And there he is, and there he stays. I've got the key in my pocket."

He displayed it.

"Did the Judge seem willin' to be shut up?" Asey asked.

"He did not! We had it hot and heavy when he found out what I planned to do with him. We—well, I'm sorry to say, I had to carry him the last few feet, bodily. But as I told him, if there was anything going on that was too dangerous for me, it was certainly just as dangerous for him. And—"

"Whyn't you call Asey?" Cummings demanded. "I should have—"

"I did, but our line's out of order," Evan said. "It's dead. This damn fog, it always seems to get that phone out of order. So I started over to Marian's—she's got the phone nearest to us. And then, as I started down the lane, I saw—"

"Banbury!" Dr. Cummings said.

"No, no, he came lots later. Hours later. This fellow ran when he heard me, and I chased him, and it turned out to be that fellow they call Rolling Reuben—"

"I know him," Cummings said. "He's a half-wit, and he's supposed to be a Peeping Tom."

"Apparently he'd been peeping," Evan said. "He just chattered around, so I let him go. Then I went back to Marian's, and called to her. But she didn't answer, so I went around to the back door and rattled it—"

"Did you think at all," Asey inquired, "of the effect of that rattlin' back door on Marian?"

"I've rattled that back door since I was knee high," Evan said. "What do you think, I was going to her front door and ring the bell like a brush salesman? Or bang her knocker? I always yell to her and rattle. Well, then I rattled the cellar window, and then I began to get worried. I began to wonder if there was something the matter, because I was sure I saw someone in the house. I wondered if a prowler'd got in, or if something was wrong, so I climbed up the trellis—"

"An' got boilin' water an' pepper hurled at you for your pains," Asey said. "Yup. I know."

"And you told me a tea kettle tipped!" Mrs. Cummings said. "You even described the kettle!"

"I didn't think," Evan said, "that you'd feel as kindly toward me, Mrs. C., if I told you I'd got it in the neck on Marian's trellis. You might have thought evil things. Anyway, Marian threw boiling water all over me—"

"How medieval of her!" Cummings said. "Did you give her hell?"

"I didn't stop to," Evan said. "When a woman is pouring boiling, scalding water all over you, you don't pause to pass the time of day and get scalded some more. It occurred to me, then, that I'd probably frightened her, rattling around, and she still didn't know who I was—"

"Whyn't you tell her?" Asey demanded. "Why didn't you yell an' tell her?"

Evan smiled from under his bandages.

"I thought it was funny," he said. "All my life I've tried to tease Marian, and I never could. And here she was, throwing boiling water at me—I just couldn't let the opportunity go. I decided to rattle about some more—I thought more rattling would pay her back for the way my neck was beginning to feel. And then tell her. But before I got the chance to tell, I turned and saw this man coming at me through the fog—"

"You poor boy!" Mrs. Cummings said.

"I'm the poor boy," Asey said. "I'm the guy he hit. An' I never came at you. You come straight for me."

Evan stared at him.

"Sure," Asey said, "it was me whose teeth you 'most jolted out. I chased you, an' you stumbled over Marian's picket fence—exactly what was you runnin' for, Evan?"

The silence that followed his question did not surprise Asey. If Evan could find a good answer to that, Evan was going to require a good, thoughtful silence.

"Well," Evan said slowly, at last, "you'll never believe me, but I was running away after you."

"Away from him, you mean, don't you?" Cummings asked.

"No. After. I thought, if I could make this man chase me, I could get him to follow me over to your house, Asey."

"By George," Cummings said blankly, "what perfectly amazing things people think! That's the last thing that would ever have occurred to me! Why, you had Asey—you'd knocked him down—"

"But I didn't know it was Asey. In the fog—"

"Even if you didn't recognize him, you knew the man was someone who had no business to be there, under the circumstances," Cummings persisted. "You knocked him down—and then you thought he'd chase you all the way over to Asey's? How? On foot? Was it an extended game of tag that you contemplated?"

"I remembered that I'd heard a car," Evan said, "and I decided that the man came in one. So I cut across the lane and got mine. I thought he'd chase me in his car, d'you see, doctor?"

Asey wished that more of Evan's face were visible. He felt sure that Evan could never have come out from behind his bandages and told such a yarn.

"Tell me, Evan," he said, "were you often shut up in that eaves closet, when you was a kid? I mean, have you always been able to lie so easy an' fluent? You're the first Chase I ever knew that was a liar."

Evan stubbed out a cigarette with great care.

"Sock," he said. "I always heard you couldn't bluff a Mayo. Well, Asey, I didn't recognize you, at first. As I went for you, I did. There was something about the angle of your yachting cap, and your silhouette in the fog. I knew it was you. So I pushed you over and beat it."

"Okay," Asey said. "Now, we're gettin' down to simple logic. I thought you was aimin' to phone me, an' that was why you went to Marian's. There I was, but you pushed me down an' beat it. They don't jibe, Evan."

"Yes, they do," Evan said. "It's one thing to summon you by phone in a dignified way, Asey, and request you to come talk sense to my uncle. And it's something else again for you to find me lurking in Marian's hydrangeas. I thought that out as I flew through the air at you. And at that point, I couldn't stop. And after I hit you, I could hardly help you up, and brush you off, and say, fancy meeting you here, I was hunting you! Now, could I? It seemed to me that my position was definitely embarrassing."

"I wonder," Cummings said, "that you brought the matter up, Evan. Why'd you tell us about the man, if you knew it was Asey?"

"Thanks, doc," Asey said. "I was just gettin' to that."

"Well," Evan said, "I guess it just comes of being one of the truthful Chase family. I should have deleted that part, but I never thought to. Besides, Asey, you didn't jump at me right off the bat, the minute I came to, and ask me—oh, I see. Giving me rope, were you?"

Asey nodded. "An' I must say, you wound it 'round yourself. Evan, I don't see why you didn't explain to me, there at Marian's. It might of been easier to believe it there, than here an' now."

Evan sighed, and lighted another cigarette.

"I thought, after I'd driven around town a few times, that I'd probably only made matters worse, so I went back to Marian's. But there really wasn't anyone there, then. I yelled, and rang, and knocked. Then I went over to Tab's, and she said you'd taken Marian home, so I went back again, just as the light went out in Marian's bedroom. Then I drove to your house, Asey, and there was no one there but a lot of cops, and your housekeeper, and none of 'em knew where you were. And about that time, my neck was hurting so, I stopped off here, and Mrs. C fixed it for me. I had fog trouble and a flat, on the way home, and I pulled up just as the town clock struck five—"

"And there was Banbury," Cummings said. "My God, I never thought we'd get to him. Now, what happened then?"

"As I drove in, Banbury came out of the fog and began to bang our knocker. I rushed up to him— I thought he was in jail, Asey!"

"He was. Go on."

"Well, Banbury looked at me and said, 'So it's you, Evan? I'm going to knock your block off. Why didn't you tell? Why didn't you do something?'"

"What did he mean?" Cummings asked.

"That's just what I asked him," Evan said. "He said I knew what he meant, and that I hadn't told, or done anything about it, and because I hadn't, his wife and daughter were going to be arrested. Then he told me to put up my hands, because he was going to knock my block off."

"Wa-el," Asey said, surveying Evan's bandages, "I think that was a reason'bly accurate statement. He didn't get it quite off, but he done a good, workman-like job. Why'd you let him? Is it an ole Chase adage never to punch your prospective father-in-law?"

"I'm not wishing you any hard luck, Asey," Evan said, "but some day I hope you have the opportunity of watching Phineas Banbury go into action. Jane had said things about popsie when he got mad, but I just thought that was her usual exaggeration. Asey, I didn't *let* Banbury do this. He did it."

"Listen," Asey said, "you jolted me—"

"Yes, but you didn't expect it! Neither did I expect what came from Banbury. After the first two wallops, I tried to get going and defend myself, but I couldn't do it. That man just pounded me down the steps, and across the lawn and into the gutter—d'you know, once he lifted me above his head and waved me around, like a dog with a rat? Believe it or not, that's what happened. And," Evan added, "if I can ever persuade Jane to marry me, we're never going to live with Banbury! I yield to no one in my admiration for Phineas Banbury, even now. But I'd never feel safe in the same house with him—"

"And you don't know why he did this?" Cummings asked.

"No, I only know he did it. Asey, I feel up to moving—let's go see uncle and pump him, and find out what he knows. Have you any idea what he's hunting, or what he's after?"

"It ought to be Abner's watch," Asey said. "Huh. One thing more, how'd you get over here? I don't see your car —an' you never could of drove yourself!"

Evan shrugged.

"I was going to ask you about that. The last I remember is the gutter."

"Asey," Cummings said, "I bet Banbury brought Evan here, himself! Evan, your car was outside the house in Weesit? Asey, that's just what happened. Banbury drove him here, left him, and went off—"

"Doubtless turning the other cheek, or something," Evan got unsteadily to his feet. "Asey, d'you know what bothers me most? How'll I ever explain this to Jane?"

"I'd advise your telling the truth," Asey said. "Your soaring into fiction ain't so hot. Here, gimme your arm. We'll go see the Judge—"

After Evan was helped into the car, Cummings called Asey back into the house.

my right eye, and my mouth feels better, and as
y wears on, I think I'll be able to move my head
And I certainly hope I can find that bridge—it
to me as though I lisped. Oh, Asey, how I feel
matter! I want to find uncle, that's all that matters."
stumbled twice as they descended the attic stairs.
inclined to think that bed is the place for you,"
aid. "You took quite a batterin'—"
y to put me to bed!" Evan returned indignantly. "Just
h, my God, look at this fog! Where can we begin,
is pea soup covering everything?"
y thought for a moment. "The Judge's already been
bog, ain't he? Huh. We'll try Abner's, then."
up on Main Street, Asey parked his car in front of
ug store.
is," he announced, "is goin' to be a brief pause for
ast— "
I never see food again," Evan told him, "it'll be all
with me. Asey, you can't guess how my mouth

aybe not," Asey said, "but I know how your face
You're goin' to have a tasty little meal of aspirin an'
through a straw. Don't argue. It won't take five
s."
the time Evan had laboriously swallowed a paper
ner of coffee, Asey was through his own breakfast.
ere," Asey dropped a handful of candy bars on the
t, "you look better, an' I feel better, an' it—"
broke off abruptly.
an, dressed in dungarees and a blue flannel zippered
had just set down a wheelbarrow on the pavement
e the drug store.
at are you watching over there?" Evan inquired
s the side I can't turn and look out of, you know."
ch, Asey thought, was just as well.
, excuse me a second, will you, Evan?" he said
, getting out of the car. "Eat a chocolate bar, o
hing. I'll be right back. I want to see that fellow
he goes—"
ay," Evan said.
leaned back against the seat, and closed his eye
wanted to find his uncle, but the way his hea
ed and pounded, he didn't care how many fellow

"D'you believe him, Asey?"

"The Chase family," Asey said cryptically, "are bad liars. They always was."

"Wait—one thing more. Will you leave this package at Tabitha's? Old Mr. Abbott's going home today, and this is a bottle of his favorite indigestion pills. I promised to leave 'em yesterday, but in the shuffle, I forgot—"

"I'll take 'em," Asey said. "He'll need 'em, too, because he's havin' a sea clam pie for a special, final lunch before he goes. I was there at the arrival of the clams."

In Weesit, over in Tabitha's kitchen, he found Mary, Marian, Tabitha and another maid, all bustling around.

"Pills for Mr. Abbott," Asey said, holding out the package. "You seem busy—"

"This Stayer," Tabitha said wearily, "has done something to the plumbing, and something else to the electric stove—it that all, Asey? You looked so purposeful, coming up the walk!"

"That's the expression you get," Asey said, "from interrupted sleep— Is your coal range goin' all right? Aha, I see you got the sea clam pie started, too. Well, I'll drop by later an' fix up the electric stove for you."

As they swung into the driveway of Judge Chase's house, Evan pointed toward the garage.

"Banbury did take my car!" he said. "See, it's gone! Asey, be gentle with uncle, but be firm, won't you? I can't let him run around, mixing himself up in anything dangerous. I'm too fond of the old fellow—"

Asey waited on the attic landing while Evan undid the bolt and unlocked the door of the eaves closet.

But the Judge was not inside.

CHAPTER XIII

EVAN LOOKED FROM THE closet to Asey, and then he sat down limply on the easy chair.

"You saw me undo those bolts! You saw me unlock— of course, he might have had a key that fitted, but he couldn't have undone those bolts! He couldn't have got out that pin prick of a window! Asey, I put that man in here—where is he?"

"Look beyond," Asey said, "at them floor boards over yonder. See—"

"You don't mean he pulled the floor up!"

"He didn't have to," Asey said, "them boards was already up. They was just fitted in, not nailed down. Don't you see, Evan, all he had to do was to lift them boards up, an' there's a nice little alley leadin' right through, under the partition, to the other eaves closet, where there ain't no bolts an' locks—"

Evan got up from the chair.

"Asey, you mean he wriggled in that space between the ceiling of the floor below and this floor up here—of course he must have, there's room enough, and the boards are crooked. Asey, how did you know? I never knew those boards were fitted!"

"Same thing in my attic at home," Asey said. "They used to use that space for storage, in the old days. My grandmother used to keep her flower seeds in tin cans, in ours. How much did the Judge fuss about bein' put up here?"

"Violently."

Asey nodded.

"An' the more he protested, the m got about puttin' him here, huh? An' l you was sure he couldn't ever get ou planned—"

"But I never knew about those floor

"Maybe you didn't," Asey said, "bu he was a boy himself, in this house. I up in the eaves closet, just like you d this."

Evan sat down again.

"I didn't think I could feel any wo seems I can. I don't like it at all— Where is he? What's he up to? Wh Why has he kept it all from me, anywa

"Whatever he knows," Asey said, " ous to know it, so he's tryin' to kee don't want anyone to think you know he didn't tell you. So—"

"What's he after?"

Asey pushed one of the floor boards

"Somebody," he said, "is huntin' A bog for somethin'. My guess is Abne ask me why anyone wants Abner's y why. But if you found the Judge on that he's huntin' that watch, too."

"Why didn't he tell me? Or you?"

"Perhaps," Asey said, "he thinks he' of gettin' to it first. I think I get his r knows that Abner's watch is somethi hunted, they'll all hunt. An' the fello he'll hunt harder, an' maybe find it soc got any thoughts about Abner's watch?

"You mean, the one Banbury gav said, "I've seen it. Abner showed it to sand times the first week he got it, It's watch, and it's got an inscription on the most prized possession, but I don't se got to do with his being killed—Asey, v we've got to find him!"

"We will—d'you feel equal to huntir

Evan got up again from the chair.

"I'm perfectly all right," he said. "I

Asey paused to see. The Porter sixteen admittedly rode like a feather on wheels, but motion of any sort was torture.

So Evan failed to witness the little scene as the man in dungarees emerged from the drug store and picked up his wheelbarrow again.

"Banbury," Asey said, "wheel that thing beyond the railroad tracks, an' I'll pick you up there!"

"Hiyah, Asey," Banbury said in the purest Cape Cod twang.

Casually, he turned the barrow around toward the tracks.

Asey watched his progress along Main Street. The nerve of the man, he thought! Marching down the main street, in full view of a good two dozen of Weesit's citizens, in full view of the cop on the corner—and there was even one of Farley's men strolling along past the movie house.

On the other hand, Banbury in dungarees and a zipper jacket and a stubble of beard bore little outward resemblance to Banbury in white flannels in a town car. And the man even had a Cape twang to his voice.

Asey watched him thoughtfully. Then he returned to the car.

Evan was asleep. And that, Asey thought, was still just as well.

Banbury was waiting beyond the tracks.

"Asey," he said, "where are Jane and Lu? Dammit, every time I call the house, no one answers but some cop—where are they?"

"They're perfectly all right," Asey said. "Banbury, what in—in the name of all that's reasonable an' logical have you been up to? What's your idea?"

"Right now," Banbury said, "I'm trying to find Judge Chase, and by George, I wish I knew where he was—have you seen him?"

"What do you want him for?"

"He sent me this message at the jail," Banbury said, "that he would settle everything. Then Farley came swaggering in, saying he was going to arrest Lu and Jane—and I couldn't take that, Asey! If the Judge knew anything, I wasn't going to have Lu and Jane dragged into this! In fact, I wasn't going to have them dragged in, anyway! So, I left. And now—"

"How'd you leave?"

"Oh, a sort of guard up there, he used to buy tarts from

my first bakery," Banbury said. "I don't know how he ever landed there, but we recognized each other. I got out, all right. I got a fellow that used to be a rum runner to ferry me down here. He landed me over in Weesit— I left a note at Dr. Cummings'. Asey, where's the Judge?"

"You think he knows somethin', huh?"

"I'm sure he knows everything. I was afraid he'd dally around and wait too long—he's a judicial sort, and he'd weigh all the pros and cons before he told you or Farley anything. I was afraid he'd wait too long—"

"What do you mean, too long?"

"Why," Banbury said, "so long that Farley'd arrest Jane and Lu, of course! So I came over to find the Judge and get him started. And I wish to God I could find the man!"

Asey looked at him a moment.

"Come over to the car," he said.

Banbury shook his head gravely at the sight of Evan, under his bandages. He sighed as Evan, waking suddenly, stared back at him.

"Evan," Banbury said apologetically, "I'm afraid I was a little hasty."

"If that's what you call a little haste," Asey observed, "I should hate to see what you could do in a tearin' hurry. What was your idea in grindin' Evan to mincemeat, did you think the Judge had told him what he knew?"

Banbury nodded. "I was so mad, by the time I reached Chase's house—this damn fog, and that stupid milkman. And I couldn't find anyone but cops at your house. So when I found Evan, I—well, Evan, I'm sorry. Maybe the Judge didn't tell you. I decided later that must be it. I'm awfully sorry, Evan. I—"

"Why did you take him over to the doc's?" Asey inquired. "Remorse?"

"He looked bad," Banbury said. "But he looks worse, now, with those bandages. I have to watch that temper of mine. Lu usually keeps me in hand— Evan, I'm sorry. I thought you knew. I can't explain, but when I saw you, and thought of Lu and Jane, something just snapped. Evan, would you like to design me this house I'm going to build in California?"

"California?" Evan said. "Why?"

"It's the farthest place I can think of from Cape Cod, right now," Banbury said. "Evan, where is your uncle?"

"Asey and I are trying to find him—say, what did you do with my car? Where is it?"

"I drove it back to your house, after I took you to Dr. Cummings'," Banbury said. "Honest, I'm sorry for what I did, Evan. But at least I took you to the doctor's. I knew that his wife would see you got fixed up. Yes, I left your car at your place. I thought I'd be better off on foot —"

"Maybe the Judge's got it," Asey suggested to Evan.

"I suppose so—but he hates to drive, and he doesn't like my car— Banbury, is that *our* wheelbarrow you've got? It is! And that's uncle's fishing coat—"

"And your pants," Banbury said. "Yes, I swiped 'em from your barn when I took the car back. I thought I ought to change. They're a pretty tight fit, but they've held out so far. Asey," Banbury opened the car door, "if you're hunting the Judge, too, let's get on with it and find him—mind if we leave your barrow here, Evan? Asey, let's get going!"

Shortly after noon, Asey parked his car on the far side of Tabitha's orchard.

"You two wait here," he told Banbury and Evan as he took a thermos bottle from a door compartment, "you wait right here, while I see if Tab knows anythin'. Don't get out, either of you. An' I'll touch Tab for some food. I think Evan's in the market for a bowl of soup."

"Make it two," Banbury suggested. "Now I think of it, I haven't eaten since yesterday noon—there's been so much else to do, I forgot about eating."

People were still bustling around Tabitha's kitchen when Asey entered.

"Hi," he said. "Got any of that sea clam pie left?"

Tabitha looked at him reproachfully.

"I never thought, Asey, that you'd do a thing like that! Stealing old Mr. Abbott's sea clam pie! We've fried him some clam cakes, but he just doesn't feel the same way about clam cakes. He'd counted on that pie. He always has one for lunch the day he leaves! And we couldn't find Freddy to get more sea clams—"

"What're you talkin' about, Tab?" Asey said. "You ain't standin' there suggestin' in all seriousness that I stole your sea clam pie, are you?"

"Didn't you?"

"I certainly did not!"

"Well, then," Tabitha said, "who did steal that sea clam pie? Who stole it, Asey? It was put right there in the pantry, and someone reached in and stole it! Now, who stole that sea clam pie?"

Asey drew a long breath. He felt suddenly very tired.

"Tabitha," he said, "don't try me. Please don't try me. I've had a very tryin' twenty-four hours, Tabitha, scamperin' around from pillar to post, an' from post to pillar. Just the Banbury family alone has tried me 'most to death. Syl has tried me. Everybody's tried me. An' now you want to know who stole your sea clam pie!"

"Why, I'm sorry, Asey," Tabitha said gently. "I'm sure I didn't mean to try you. But Mary said that you joked about Freddy and the clams last night, and you made some comment about the pie when you came marching in here this morning with those pills—I thought you might—well, it doesn't matter. Do you want some coffee in your thermos?"

"Soup," Asey said.

"There's chowder," Mary said. "Sit right down and I'll fix up some—"

"I'll have chowder," Asey said, "but I want soup in the thermos. Wouldn't you have some chicken broth?"

Tabitha's eyes narrowed. So Asey was going to have chowder, but he wanted chicken broth, too.

"Asey," she said, "you wouldn't want me to throw together a sort of picnic lunch, would you? To take along with you?"

"I think," Asey said, "that'd be real nice. Never can tell when I might meet some starvin' wayfarer. Thanks, Tab."

Tabitha smiled as she hastily made sandwiches in the pantry. She thought she knew now the answer to the disappearance of her sea clam pie. Asey had found Phineas Banbury, and Banbury was still hungry, even after taking the sea clam pie. She had had considerable experience with Phineas Banbury's appetite.

"Well, Mrs. Milton," Asey split a Boston cracker and dropped it in his chowder, "you didn't hear no more prowlers last night, did you?"

"We didn't hear a thing," Mary said. "I can't see what got Marian and Tabitha so frightened. I never heard a sound."

Asey chuckled. "You was sleepin' sound enough when I crawled up that trellis—"

"You didn't!" Marian said. "Asey, did you climb that trellis? How lucky for you I never heard you! I had a bucket of water by my bed, and a flounder spear we found in the shed!"

Ten minutes later, armed with a hamper and a thermos, Asey returned to the car.

"I think," he told Banbury, "that Tabitha's resigned to it on your account, but you're goin' to have to sit down an' write a letter of apology to poor ole Mr. Abbott for stealin' that sea clam pie of his. Here—"

"Sandwiches!" Banbury said. "Ah, Tabitha guessed I was around, didn't she? Deviled ham and pickle, she knows I like those—what's this about a sea clam pie?"

"Didn't you steal Mr. Abbott's sea clam pie from Tab's pantry?"

"I never stole a sea clam pie in my life!" Banbury said with his mouth full. "I think sea clam pies are terrible. I ate some to be polite, when Tabitha had one, one day. But I thought it was terrible! If she thinks I'd steal one of the things, she's crazy! If I was starving, I wouldn't steal a sea clam pie."

"What he means," Evan said as Asey presented him with a cup of chicken soup, "is that someone else stole the sea clam pie—what a funny thing to steal! Why did Tabitha think Phineas stole it?"

Asey shrugged.

"I suppose," Banbury said, "I'll be blamed for anything that happens around this town from now on—I just hope it won't be for anything worse than a sea clam pie. Asey, did Tabitha know anything about the Judge? I'm beginning to worry about him!"

"So am I," Evan said. "Asey, what about going to Farley? Shouldn't we ask him to help us find uncle?"

"No," Banbury said. "With all this fog, I don't think Farley can do any more than we're doing. If you ask me, I don't think Farley could find the nose on his own face, without outside aid—why, he can't even find me, and I walked right past him this morning, with your wheelbarrow! And, anyway, I don't think you'd better give me any opportunity of losing my temper at him, till Lu's around to hold me back. Could Farley do more, Asey? And don't you suppose the Judge must have gone off somewhere, in Evan's car? That must be the answer."

"Maybe," Asey said.

Evan put down his empty soup cup.

"Asey, I'm really worried! Let's hunt—"

All three of them were more than worried when evening came without their finding any trace whatsoever of the Judge.

"An' East Weesit, an' the Center, an' the village," Asey finished ticking off on his fingers the places where they had been. "I don't know where else to go. We covered every part of town, an' pretty soon Farley's goin' to begin trailin' this car."

"Why in thunder do you think the Judge is hunting Abner's watch?" Banbury asked.

"I've told you I don't know," Asey said wearily. "It just seems to fill the bill. Look, I forgot to ask you—what about the cane the selectmen gave you? Where is it?"

"Lord, I don't know! Lu might, though. I've got a barrel of canes, and Lu always sees to it that the right one is out for the right people to see—did I ever show you that sword cane, Evan? That's one I always liked—"

"An' where," Asey said, "was that arsenic in the cellar?"

"Oh, in that little work room where I've got that saw," Banbury said. "Evan fixed me up a little work room down there. I thought I might make model ships or something, but I never had the time—"

"I know what you're driving at, Asey," Evan said. "The work room's at the foot of the stairs, and easily accessible. You go past the door on the way to the heating plant—er —how many people have you showed that heating plant to, Phineas?"

"Everyone," Banbury said. "That's a fine heating plant, Asey. I must show it to you some day."

"If you must," Asey said, "I suppose you must. Huh, you certainly made things easy for people, Banbury, strewin' canes around an' cartin' everyone through the cellar where the arsenic was. An' then beatin' it out of jail, an' roamin' around—you don't care how wide open you leave things, do you?"

"My wife and my daughter," Banbury said, "mean—"

"Yup. I know. I'm goin' to get 'em now," Asey told him,

"an' I'm goin' to leave them an' you an' Evan over at the doc's. An'—"

"I'm going to find uncle!" Evan said.

"I'm going to find the Judge!" Banbury announced.

"If I have to help the doc to chloroform you," Asey said, "you are all stayin' at his place."

Turning a deaf ear to their objections, Asey drove them over to Wellfleet and the "Emily."

Mrs. Banbury greeted her husband tranquilly.

"You need a shave, dear—oh, my! Is that Evan? Jane, look at Evan! Phineas Banbury, did you do that?"

"Well," Banbury said, "I was a little hasty—"

"Evan, you poor thing!" Jane said. "Popsie, how could you have? It's disgraceful. It's—"

"I don't think he's as bad as the fake prince," Mrs. Banbury said, critically. "Or that lifeguard—"

"Maybe not," Jane said, "but you'll pay through the nose for this, popsie. This wedding is going to cost you plenty!"

"My God!" Banbury said. "You mean—but I thought you thought he had one foot in the grave!"

"That's no reason," Jane retorted, "for your trying to shove the other in—"

"Would you mind postponin' all this," Asey said, "till you get to the doc's? Syl, what's that you got! Is that that tarnation clock?"

"That reminds me, speaking of clocks," Mrs. Banbury said, "have you ever found the watch of Abner's that we started to scour and comb for? Do you think someone stole it?"

"That's nothing," Banbury said, "he and Tabitha think I've stolen a sea clam pie!"

Asey winced.

"Sometimes," he said in a calm voice, "a man gets tried beyond endurance—git to the doctor's, all of you, an' git there quick!"

Dr. and Mrs. Cummings promised him faithfully that they would keep the Banburys and Evan safe and sound. Mrs. Banbury promised him that she would not let Phineas out of her sight.

"And I know Jane will look after Evan—you know, everything turns out for the best, doesn't it? I'd been wondering how much longer it would take them to break the news to us, and so had Phineas, and now everything's all cleared up!"

"That," Asey said, "is one way of lookin' at it."

After a hasty supper, Asey went out to his car. Syl was sitting inside, holding Abner's clock in his lap.

"No!" Asey said. "Get out. Take that clock with you—"

"Just drop me off, Asey," Syl said, "somewhere near Abner's, that's all. Ain't goin' over to Abner's anyways? I thought so. Let me go along. Say, Asey, I still don't understand about that clock—"

Syl was still discussing the clock when they reached Abner Grove's house.

"I'm goin' to put that clock up," he said, "an' then I'm goin' to set an' watch it an' find out why it stops— ain't you comin' in, Asey? You just goin' to sit there in the car?"

"Scat!" Asey said.

He was still sitting in the car when Syl came out of the house ten minutes later.

"It works fine, Asey," he said. "I put it up, an' it works —what you sittin' here for? What's the matter?"

"Smell," Asey said. "What do you smell?"

Syl sniffed.

"Fog. Fog, an' the tide."

"Listen," Asey said. "What do you hear?"

"Tide comin' in—"

"An' why? Why'd the tide be comin' in this meadow for? I can't see it, but I can hear it an' smell it," Asey said. "That meadow's flooded."

"There's always high tides the last part of August," Syl said. "It's just a regular high tide—maybe the culvert clapper's stuck, huh?"

"Is there a culvert? Where? Get in this car, Syl! Where?"

"Well, I sort of want to watch that clock—"

"Get in, Syl. Where's the culvert?"

"On the tarred road beyond the turn of this lane," Syl said. "Same kind of culvert we got home in Wellfleet, Asey, with a leather clapper. Drains the meadow at low tide, an' shuts up when the tides comes in—you think the clapper's stuck?"

"I'm 'fraid," Asey said grimly, "that it's more than stuck, Syl!"

They found the tide pouring through the culvert into the meadow.

"Grab that flash, Syl," Asey said. "Come on—"

Syl followed him down the banking.

Fifteen minutes later, the two of them, soaked to their skins, clambered back up the banking onto the road.

Syl shook the water from his dripping clothes.

"Well," he said, "it's all right now, an' Weesit ought to give us a vote of thanks— Asey, why'n time would anyone want to prop that clapper open an' flood this meadow on purpose?"

"Come along," Asey got into the car. "Hurry—"

"You'll spoil that nice leather seat, Asey, drippin' over it—"

"Hurry!" Asey said. "We'll get some dry things at Abner's an' then you an' I'll find out why someone's floodin' this meadow. We been here a dozen times today, yellin' around for the Judge, but this time, we'll—we'll *scour* this meadow!"

Around eleven o'clock that night, Syl and Asey found Judge Chase.

Beyond him on the edge of the meadow was Evan's car, parked in the bushes. Beside him lay Phineas Banbury's sword cane.

But, like Abner Grove, the Judge had been drowned.

CHAPTER XIV

ASEY DID NOT NEED THE aid of Dr. Cummings to know that the Judge had been drowned.

He had to have been drowned. His face was submerged in the stream that ran through the meadow.

And, Asey thought, if he and Syl had not attended to the culvert clapper, the body would eventually have washed out with the tide, when it ebbed.

Someone had set the scene in case the Judge's body was found right there where they had found it. But, after the tide went out—

Syl echoed Asey's thoughts.

"I bet," he said, "he'd have floated out. That culvert's big enough an' wide enough—hold the light over, Asey. Say, what hit him on the back of the head? Was it that cane? Funny cane."

"It's a sword cane," Asey said. "An' it belongs to Banbury. There's somethin' engraved on the knob. The funny part, Syl, is that they didn't use the sword, but the cane. Huh. Well, I suppose when you commit what seems to be one successful murder, there ain't no reason for you to change your method in the next. If it worked once, it'll work again."

"Why was he killed?" Syl asked. "Why would anyone kill the Judge?"

"I think," Asey said slowly, "that he found the watch that I think he was huntin' for. An' I think that someone was watchin' for him to find it. When he did, they was waitin' to take it away from him. P'raps they found it first, an' he tried to get it from them. Anyway, I see where he didn't want to tell Evan anything. He knew that if Evan hunted, there was danger in it for him."

"That's Evan's car," Syl said.

Asey nodded. "Evan's car, that he drove 'round, an' Banbury drove 'round. An' that's Banbury's cane—"

"With this happenin' after Banbury escaped from jail," Syl said, "you know what I bet? I bet Farley will claim that Banbury's responsible for this, too."

"I just bet," Asey agreed with a smile, "that he does. It's just what he's supposed to bet. Syl, this is Farley's business, now. I'll go back to the house an' phone for him. You stay here. Say, we're near Abner's—I didn't realize how near, we been twistin' an' turnin' around so."

"It's this fog," Syl said. "I don't know why, Asey, but it always seemed to me that the fog in this town was always thicker than it was any other place. What you thinkin' about?" he added, as Asey paused and looked again at the still figure on the meadow.

"Thinkin'," Asey said, "of what the Judge said, over to my house yesterday mornin'. He said that there wasn't no threat that meant more to him than his town. Yes, Syl, he found that watch. I'm sure he did. I only wish I knew why he thought it was important."

Syl considered for a moment. "Might be a picture in it," he said at last. "You know how people stick pictures in watches. Why, I still got a picture of Jennie when she was eighteen, in mine. Think it could be a picture, like of the murderer?"

"No," Asey said. "I hardly think so. But you opened up a whole new train of thought for me, Syl—you stay here till Farley or his men come."

"Okay. Say, Asey," Syl called after him as he left, "take a look at that clock for me, will you? Look an' see if it's still goin'?"

Asey grinned, and picked his way, by the aid of his flashlight, across the meadow to Abner's house.

He went directly to the desk in the dining room.

Syl's suggestion about the picture had made him think of something he had seen in a pigeon hole earlier in the day. Something he hadn't given a thought to, at the time.

It was still in the pigeon hole, that box of onion skin

paper. And there were scissors on the desk. And, on the floor, were snipped pieces of the onion skin paper. And, in the fireplace— Asey smiled as he knelt on the hearth. In the fireplace were pieces of the onion skin paper, with circles cut out of them.

"A round, gold watch," someone had told him.

Asey sat down and pulled out his pipe.

It wasn't possible that Abner had written things on the onion skin circles that he had cut out, and then put them in his watch.

"But why not?" Asey said to himself. "After all, why not? People put pictures in their watches. Why shouldn't they put papers in, too?"

You might call it vanity if you wanted to, Asey decided. If Abner had little papers in his watch, Abner would have to display the watch to get the papers out. And there wasn't anyone who hadn't mentioned how proud Abner was of that watch.

Or you could take it from another angle. Abner had no safe in the house, and he probably didn't own a box in the bank vault. It was possible that he might have used his watch as a sort of miniature safe.

Asey went to the phone.

"I want Tabitha Sparrow," he said. "What? Oh, hang! Wait'll I look the number up, then!"

The machine age, Asey thought as he thumbed through the phone book, had come to Weesit with the new operator.

He finally succeeded in getting Tabitha, by number.

"Certainly, I'll come over to Abner's," she said in response to his question. "Yes, at once. Right away."

Asey replaced the receiver and cranked the bell.

"Now," he said to the phone girl, "I want Farley, the police officer, and I don't know his number, an' I don't know where he is. Nope, I got no fuller information as to his whereabouts. This is Asey Mayo, an' I want Farley. Yup, I thought you probably could locate him."

The police officer with whom Asey spoke assured him that he would find Farley and send him to Abner Grove's.

Asey sat down to wait. The clock, he noticed, was still going on the wall, and he hoped that for his own peace of mind, Syl diagnosed the trouble with it soon. He was getting to hate that clock.

This was what his friend Bill Porter would call the Department of Utter Despair.

With a sigh, he thought back to the beginning of things. Somebody had begun by starting some propaganda against Banbury. Then they progressed to putting arsenic in the tarts, to discredit Banbury. Because Abner guessed, Abner was killed. And everything that could be done to implicate Banbury was done.

The thing, as the doctor said, had been planned, and must have been planned for some time.

But anyone could have taken Banbury's canes, apparently. Anyone could have noticed or found or taken that arsenic from the cellar. Anyone could have thrown those stones, or picked up Tabitha's pin, or taken a nail from that box in her car. Almost anyone could have put the nail in his tire, or twitched that screw out of his windshield wiper. Anyone could have made those phone calls to Tabitha and Marian. Anyone could have laid out that food in Abner's kitchen, or slammed down the trap door, or scooped along the bog for Abner's watch.

And, Asey thought, Evan's story had its loopholes. And so, heaven knew, did Banbury's. Banbury had no alibis, either for Abner's death or for Judge Chase's. He was wandering around by himself both nights, a fact of which the murderer had taken full advantage.

Asey sat up suddenly as a door opened and someone came in through the kitchen.

Breathlessly, Tabitha entered the dining room.

"I've hurried, but the fog—"

Asey stood up.

"Tabitha, go out an' shut the door, an' then come in again. Just like you did now. Quick!"

"Why—why, all right."

Obediently, she turned and left the house, then opened the door again and returned.

"What—"

"I've found out," Asey said, "what makes that clock stop! What door did you come in, the woodshed door?"

"I always do," Tabitha said. "Everyone does. Asey, what— "

"It's the draft," Asey said. "Blows in through the kitchen when that shed door's opened. Stops the pendulum. I started it again when you went out, an' it stopped when you come in. The wind's south-east—"

"Is this something important?" Tabitha asked.

"Wait now. It's south-east tonight. It was south-east Wednesday night. But it was west on Thursday mornin'— oho. The clock stopped at nine-fifteen on Wednesday night, then, an' not at nine-fifteen Thursday mornin'. Couldn't get that draft with a west wind. Now, things pick up— an'," Asey added, "now I'll never hear the end of this blessed clock!"

"I'm afraid I don't—is this what you wanted from me?" Tabitha asked in some perplexity.

"Nope, this is a side issue. Person Abner was waitin' for come at nine-fifteen. That's nice to know. Now, what I wanted to find out from you was what Abner cut little circles of onion skin paper out for. They look like they might fit a watch."

"They do," Tabitha said. "I told you, he was proud of that watch. He carried it always. And he had a habit of forgetting papers. So, a month or so ago, he decided that it would be a good idea to carry things in his watch—why, he had half a town report on two circles of paper! He showed me them!"

"Why," Asey said, "didn't you tell me!"

"You never asked, and I never thought to. I thought it was silly of him—it was just another chance for him to display that watch."

"If Abner wrote town reports an' stuck 'em in his watch," Asey said, "he could write down what he knew about the person he thought was tryin' to injure Banbury. He did. That night he was killed, he either lost his watch, him-self, out there on the meadow, or someone lost it movin' him. Later, they remembered his habit of writin' things on little circles of paper an' puttin' 'em in his watch. So they set out to hunt that watch. Judge Chase knew about that habit. P'raps Abner even said, in his vacillatin' way, that he wouldn't tell the Judge who he suspected, but he'd got it all written down. Judge Chase tried to find the watch, an' he did. An'—" Asey paused.

"Asey—oh, Asey! Not—not the Judge, too! I can tell by your face— Asey, not the Judge, too!"

"I'm sorry to tell you like this," Asey said. "I forgot you didn't know. Tab, I am sorry, don't—oh, golly, here's

Farley! Tabitha, pop into the sittin' room an' stay there till I get him out of the way—"

Farley was in the best of spirits when he entered the dining room.

"Hi, Asey," he said. "Asey, I take it all back about the doctor. Did he tell you about that cranberry scoop he found? Well, that's put a whole new angle on this. That wasn't a real scoop, but one of those imitation scoops they use for magazine stands. And it belonged to Tabitha Sparrow."

"How do you know it did?" Asey asked.

"We found out from the old fellow that makes 'em, over in East Weesit. He made that scoop specially for a boarder of Tabitha Sparrow's, out of a certain kind of wood. And the boarder gave it to her as a present. And then we found out that Tabitha Sparrow was a great friend of Grove's. And did you know that she was a relation of Banbury's?"

"What!"

"Oh, yes. Banbury came here to Weesit," Farley said, "because he had a great-uncle Phineas Knowles who came from here. This great-uncle left Banbury the money that Banbury started out in business with, and made his fortune on. See? There's your motive for getting Banbury in bad— family jealousy that the money wasn't left to the family here, see?"

"How," Asey inquired, "do you explain the scoop?"

"She can explain that," Farley said. "I'm going now to see her and—"

"Before you go into that," Asey said, "call my cousin Syl, out on the meadow, an' see what's happened—"

He told Farley, briefly, about the Judge.

Tabitha came out of the sitting room after Farley's hasty departure.

"Was the scoop yours?" Asey asked.

She nodded. "And it's been in the barn since spring house cleaning. Asey, I didn't know that Phineas' great-uncle Phin was a Knowles! And, Asey, that night I told you I was playing cribbage with old Mr. Abbott, I wasn't at all. I'm just so used to cribbage with him, I never thought that we didn't play that night. It was the night before. I've got no alibi at all for the time Abner was killed. I can't even say I went to the mail, because that was the night the mail changed. The trains stopped, you know—oh, were you home then?"

"Say that again," Asey told her curtly.

"You knew the trains stopped? And the mail comes by bus, early in the evening. The office window used to be open till nine, but now it closes at six. That was the night, Wednesday, that it changed. Wha-what are you doing?"

"Come along," Asey took her by the elbow. "Hustle, Tab. Come along—"

"Where are you— Asey, what is this? Where are you taking me?"

"To Doc Cummings'," Asey said.

"What for? What did I say? Oh, Asey, I know it all looks bad, and sounds bad, but I didn't—" Tabitha gulped. "Why there? What for?"

"Because I got things to do," Asey said, "in a big hurry. an' you know just enough so that someone might take it into their heads to do away with you—hurry—"

"But I don't know anything! All I know is that Phineas Banbury stole my sea clam pie. That's the only thing— what are you yelling about?"

"I got it," Asey told her. "I got that pie!"

"You told me you didn't take it! You said—"

"Tab, stop talkin'." Asey pushed her through the kitchen and out along the oyster shell path. "You upset my thoughts. Get into the car. Hang on—oh, who's the oldest inhabitant in Weesit? Who?"

"Freddy's grandmother, I think. She's ninety-eight— Asey, the only thing I was sure of in all this was that pie—"

"Ssh," Asey said. "I got to think."

Tabitha was smothered with questions after Asey left her at the doctor's.

"I tell you, I don't know!" she said for the twentieth time. "I don't know, Phineas. I don't know, doctor. All I know is, he found out something about a draft stopping a clock pendulum. He talked about that clock."

Mrs. Banbury sighed. "So did Syl. Endlessly."

"And about Abner's watch—"

"Momsie," Jane said, "did you hear that? That watch?"

"We told him that was a clew," Mrs. Banbury said with satisfaction. "He didn't think so, but I knew all along it was. Clocks and watches, always. I'm so glad Asey changed his mind about that. What else?"

"Did he say anything about that pie he thought I stole?" Banbury demanded.

"He said he had it," Tabitha said. "And he muttered something about garbage holes and the evening mail, and he asked me who the oldest inhabitant of Weesit was, and where she lived. Phineas, you never told me your great-uncle Phin was named Knowles! That's my family—"

"Was Asey asking things about great-uncle Phin?" Mrs. Banbury wanted to know. "Oh, Phineas! That means he's got back to you!"

"If you ask me," Evan said, "he's crazy, Asey is—why didn't he say anything about uncle?"

"He's not crazy." Dr. Cummings saved Tabitha from answering. Asey had told them both not to mention what had happened to the Judge. "I know that look on Asey's face. When he begins to purr, all you have to do is wait."

While the group still waited at Dr. Cummings', Asey got into his car outside old Mrs. Higgins'. He had worried about disturbing the old lady at that time of night, but Freddy, the clam man, assured him sleepily that his grandmother would probably be awake reading, and she was. She had answered Asey's questions briskly and efficiently, and she had cleared up a very important point. There had been two Phineas Knowleses, in the old days, and Farley had characteristically found out about the wrong one. Asey learned about the other. And he had also learned the fate of Tabitha's sea clam pie, after a rather unsavory examination of a garbage hole.

Things, Asey decided as he started the car, were picking up.

Back at the doctor's, he called for Banbury.

"Dressed? Good. I want you, I want bandages, an' mercurochrome. Hustle."

He gave no one a chance to ask questions, and he didn't even explain much to Banbury, when he stopped and bound the latter's head up with the bandages, which he dabbled with mercurochrome.

"I ought," Banbury said plaintively, "to look worse than Evan—"

"You do," Asey assured him. "I mean you to. You are the ewe lamb."

"I'm what?"

"You," Asey said, "are goin' to bleat. Banbury, someone started this business to get you. They got Abner before he told on 'em, an' they got Judge Chase before he had a chance to tell what he found out from Abner's watch, an' —"

"Not the Judge!"

"Yes. Now, they never tried to kill you. I want to give 'em a chance. Will you take one? You," Asey said, "take the direct way. That's what I want to take, now. If it works, this business is settled. I'll try to see to it that you don't get hurt. But you may."

"Shoot," Banbury said briefly. "I liked Judge Chase."

"Very well." Asey slowed down the car. "We'll walk from here—"

"Where are we? I can't tell, with all this fog."

"Weesit again. Look. I want you to walk ahead there about a hundred yards. I'll keep behind. Then I want you to fall down on your face, an' crawl. I want you to moan. If this works, someone'll come. Then you pretend to collapse, you're so done up. I'll do the rest."

Banbury's groans as he crawled along at the end of the hundred yards were so realistic that they made Asey shudder.

He ducked behind a bush as he saw the glow of a flashlight in the fog, and heard footsteps approaching.

Edging nearer, Asey saw the person bend over Banbury, and examine him with the flash.

Banbury's last groan before his pretended collapse was a masterpiece.

"Banbury! Banbury!"

There was something gloating about that whisper that came through the fog. Asey's fingers unconsciously tightened on his Colt.

"Banbury! I've got *you,* now!"

Something was raised above Banbury's head, and Asey's Colt barked.

A split second later, Banbury was on his feet.

"I've got her, Asey," he said. "D'you know she was going to brain me? Oh, my God, she's gone hysterical— Marian, stop it!"

Asey and Phineas Banbury, together, delivered Mrs. Milton over to Farley before she stopped being hysterical.

"If," Asey said to the bewildered officer, "you just

listen to her long enough, you'll hear the whole thing. Good night."

"I'm—I'm shattered," Banbury said, as Asey turned the car once more toward Wellfleet. "And tell me—what was that she was saying about blood? Whose blood? Your shot never hit her. It just shot that stick out of her hands that she was going to brain me with. She said something about blood, and that started her off."

"Mercurochrome," Asey said. "The doc said somethin' about her an' the sight of blood. That's why she used that sword cane as a cane, an' not a sword. Oh, she was your relation. Not Tab. Did you know that?"

"My God, no!"

"I guessed as much, with her livin' in the old Knowles place. There was two men named Phineas Knowles. Your great-uncle got staked to his trip west by some one of her relations. Old Mrs. Higgins told me so. But he left his money to you, an' not to the folks that staked him—"

"Was that why she did everything?"

"Nope," Asey said. "She tried hard to make her rug business go, an' she tried to make the town run, an' she done her best to be a big shot. Then you come along, an' you done in a month what she spent years tryin' to do. You got credit. People liked you. She never got credit, an' people didn't like her. She got sore."

"So, she swiped my canes, and some of that arsenic—did you hear her brag about that?"

"Uh-huh. Abner suspected her, see? An' because he dallied so, he got killed. Your cane an' those tubs, like I thought. That was just after nine-fifteen on Wednesday."

"What did she mean," Banbury demanded, "about her alibi?"

Asey smiled. "She primed Mary. Mary told me that she an' Marian got the mail together that night. Packages, at the window. Mary didn't think she was lyin' about it, any more than Tabitha did when Tab told me she was playin' cribbage with old Mr. Abbott that night. When you do things regular, you can get confused real easy."

"Didn't she get the mail?"

"That was the day the trains stopped. The mail time changed, after fifty years. Even I was so used to the evenin' mail, I didn't get it," Asey said, as he turned into Dr. Cummings' drive.

He had not intended to stop there, but Jane and Lu Banbury, the Cummingses and Tabitha, all seemed to swarm over the car. Evan had been forced to remain inside.

The bandages on Banbury's head nearly caused a riot, until Banbury tore them off and gave them to his wife.

"There, see? Lu, listen!"

At the conclusion of his story, Tabitha broke the silence.

"She found my pin, and put it over there at the Banburys'? And she took my scoop from the barn?"

"An' your nails from the car," Asey said. "Seems she put that nail in my tire, Jane, the same time she was bein' a delegate, with Tab an' the Judge. That's why she botched it. She was in a hurry. An' she took the screw out of my windshield wiper. An' the rocks was easy."

"She shut us in the cellar?" Mrs. Banbury asked.

"Yup. An' she opened the door that made the draft that stopped that clock Syl's been fiddlin' with. Knowin' Abner, she'd use that door. Look, she's tellin' all this over an' over again. It'll all be in tomorrow's papers—"

"She put that supper out at Abner's," Mrs. Banbury said. "Of course, that's a woman's touch. That opener by the peaches. Two tea bags."

"But last night," Tabitha said, "Mary was with her!"

"Mary said she slept sound," Asey said. "Guess why Mary slept sound? Marian did somethin' to the cup of cocoa they had to settle their nerves. Mary slept sound, but Marian didn't. Tabitha, I can see you scared of prowlers, but I couldn't see her. Evan just walked right into it for her, last night. 'Course, she guessed it was him. He always rattled things, he said. But it made you feel scared, an' it threw me off."

"But those calls!" Tabitha said. "Asey, I just can't believe that!"

"She only had to call you a few times," Asey said, "from assorted pay stations. That's all. The rest she made up. Except for ringin' the Judge's house a couple of times herself. She could do that herself, because they're on the same line. When she cut the phone line, she rooked the Judge's, too. Tabitha, don't you remember how she changed her mind suddenly, when she found out Banbury was out of jail? She saw another chance, there. Whatever she might do, Banbury'd be blamed for—"

"Like that damn pie," Banbury said. "That—"

"What about that?" Tabitha asked.

Asey grinned. "You was finishin' it when I come to your house—"

"Marching so purposefully." Tabitha said. "You frightened me. You—"

"I frightened Marian, too," Asey said. "She had that watch with her. An' I looked menacin'. So she popped it into the pie. Then she had to steal the pie when it was done, don't you see? She couldn't leave the watch in there to confuse old Mr. Abbott, could she? I found the pie in her garbage hole tonight. She was so sure of herself, she hadn't bothered to take the watch out. I gave it to Farley."

Banbury sighed. "I think—"

"Look!" Jane said. "The fog—popsie, it's going just the way it did that day in June, remember? Look! Why, I didn't know there was water over there! Dad! Look! Dawn, and that view—"

"I'm so sick of views," Banbury said. "I'm so sick of water, I swish. Lu, did you hear from Charley?"

Mrs. Banbury hadn't, but she nodded.

"He thinks," she said firmly, "that you really need that new factory. He wants you to come and see to it, yourself. Don't you think we'd better leave before Labor Day—oh, Asey—wait! Oh, he's gone, Phineas, and you never thanked him!"

"You can always," Tabitha suggested, "send him a cane. Suitably engraved."

As Asey went upstairs in his own house, Jennie called out to him sleepily.

"That you, Asey?"

"Uh-huh."

"All done over at Cranberry Bog?"

"Done," Asey said, "is right."

"Settled Mr. Cranberry—Banbury?"

"Uh-huh."

"Then for goodness' sakes," Jennie said, "put on your clean shirt before the reporters an' the photographers get here. That shirt an' that suit's been lyin' there since Thursday mornin'!"

"Uh-huh."

"Oh—how's the fog?"

"The fog has lifted," Asey said, and went to bed.